This book belongs to ...

100% UNOFFICIAL

First published in Great Britain 2026 by 100% Unofficial, a part of Farshore

An imprint of HarperCollins*Publishers*
1 London Bridge Street, London SE1 9GF
www.farshore.co.uk

HarperCollins*Publishers*
Macken House, 39/40 Mayor Street Upper,
Dublin 1 D01 C9W8 Ireland

Illustrations by Giselle Pe
Additional images used under license from Shutterstock.com

This book is an original creation by Farshore

ISBN 978 0 00 875473 0
Printed in Romania
001

ONLINE SAFETY FOR YOUNGER FANS

Spending time online is great fun! Here are a few simple rules to help younger fans stay safe and keep the internet a great place to spend time.

- Never give out your real name – don't use it as your username.
- Never give out any of your personal details.
- Never tell anybody which school you go to or how old you are.
- Never tell anybody your password, except a parent or guardian.
- Be aware that you must be 13 or over to create an account on many sites. Always check the site policy and ask a parent or guardian for permission before registering.
- Always tell a parent or guardian if something is worrying you.

Stay safe online. Any website addresses listed in this book are correct at the time of going to print. However, Farshore is not responsible for content hosted by third parties. Please be aware that online content can be subject to change and websites can contain content that is unsuitable for children. We advise that all children are supervised when using the internet.

FSC www.fsc.org
MIX
Paper | Supporting responsible forestry
FSC® C005461

100% UNOFFICIAL ROBLOX ANNUAL 2027

CONTENTS

Get ready to collect and cherish lots (and we mean LOTS) of pets, like these adorable chickens, in Egg Empire!

Set off on a wild and cosy adventure through forests with your green backpack in Backpack Adventure: Find the Animals!

Time to strut your stuff, like this model rocking a white bow and oversized brown tee, in Fashion Famous!

HELLO!

Welcome to the

100% UNOFFICIAL ROBLOX ANNUAL 2027!

Ready to celebrate another brilliantly blocky year in the world of Roblox? The 100% Unofficial Roblox Annual 2027 is here! In your hands, you hold the ultimate review of the entire Roblox universe, and we can't wait to go on this epic journey with you!

We'll be looking at the greatest experiences and games that have been most popular over the last year. Get ready to freefall into obby games, curl up with cute pet experiences, join the thrilling world of sports and experience ghastly horror games!

Plus, if you're new to Roblox, we've got a handy beginner's guide that reviews the basics, so you can decide how to get started!

As always, the most important part of playing Roblox is having fun and expressing yourself! There's never been a better time to get your game loaded, dress your avatars in your favourite outfits and jump into the action.

Are you ready? **Let's go!**

Get ready to celebrate the world of Roblox, just like these players are cheering their massive win in the game Rivals!

ROBLOX BEGINNER'S GUIDE

Every year, millions of new players create their Roblox account and start gaming. Here's a rundown of the essential information you need to know to stay safe and start your next Roblox adventure!

1 BEING SAFE ONLINE

Playing online games is so fun, but it's important to stay safe. Never give out your real name or any personal details. Plus, be wary of unknown players, especially if they propose swapping items with you – only trade with your IRL (in real life) friends!

2 THE HOME SCREEN

To set up an account, enter in your birthday, a username and a password. You can also add an email address, which is handy if you forget your password! Once you're signed up, check out the charts for the hottest games you can try straight away.

3 BOSS THE CONTROLS

Although many games have similar controls that are quick to pick up, it's always a good idea to practise. Each game will explain on their about page or loading screen the controls for walking, jumping and more. When you can control a game with your eyes closed, you can call yourself a master. But play with your eyes open, silly! Try starting off in quiet, open areas within the game (like this peaceful, woodland space with the red house above!), to master your skills.

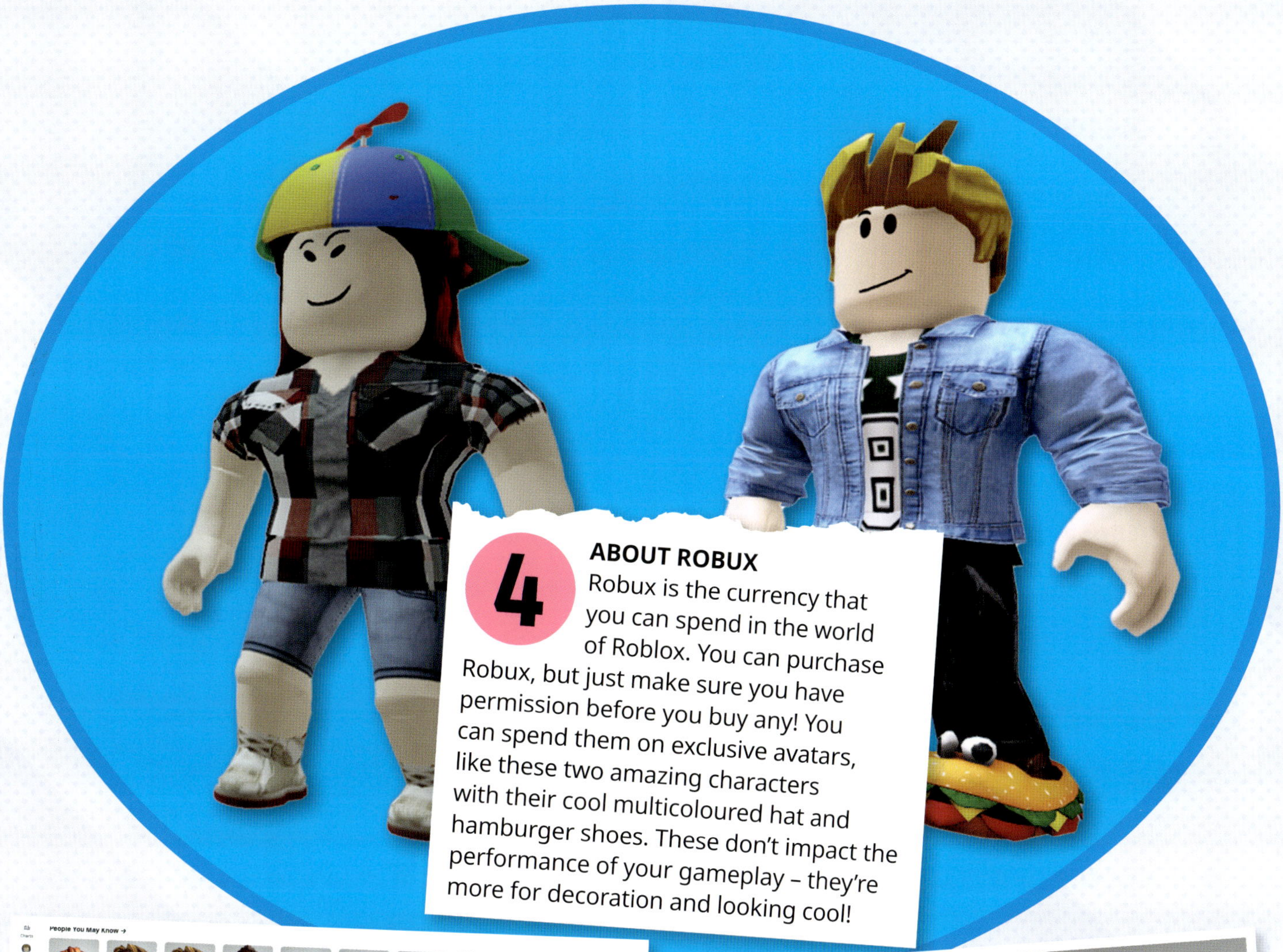

4 ABOUT ROBUX

Robux is the currency that you can spend in the world of Roblox. You can purchase Robux, but just make sure you have permission before you buy any! You can spend them on exclusive avatars, like these two amazing characters with their cool multicoloured hat and hamburger shoes. These don't impact the performance of your gameplay – they're more for decoration and looking cool!

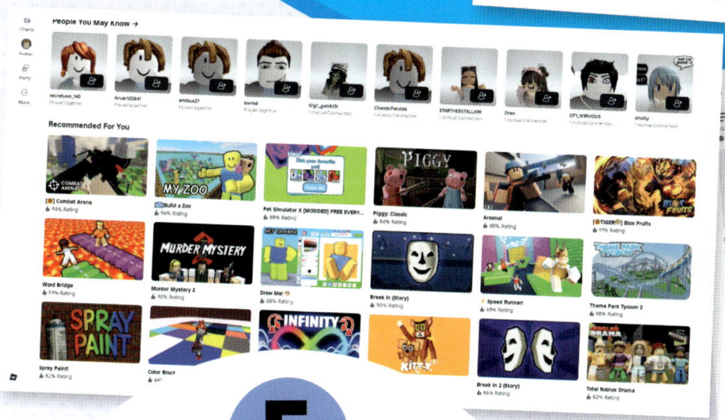

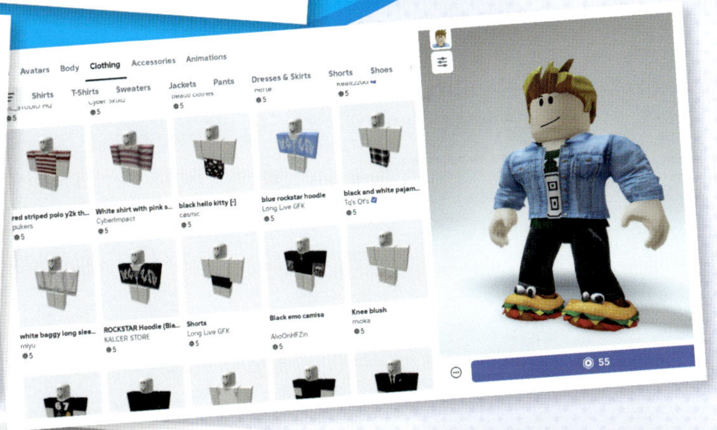

5 AWESOME AVATARS

One of the coolest things about Roblox is the customisation options on offer. Games have their own unique items that you can unlock or purchase using Robux. The Roblox Marketplace Catalogue has avatars, clothes and accessories, and lots of them are free! Use the filters and enter 0 min and 0 max to show free items.

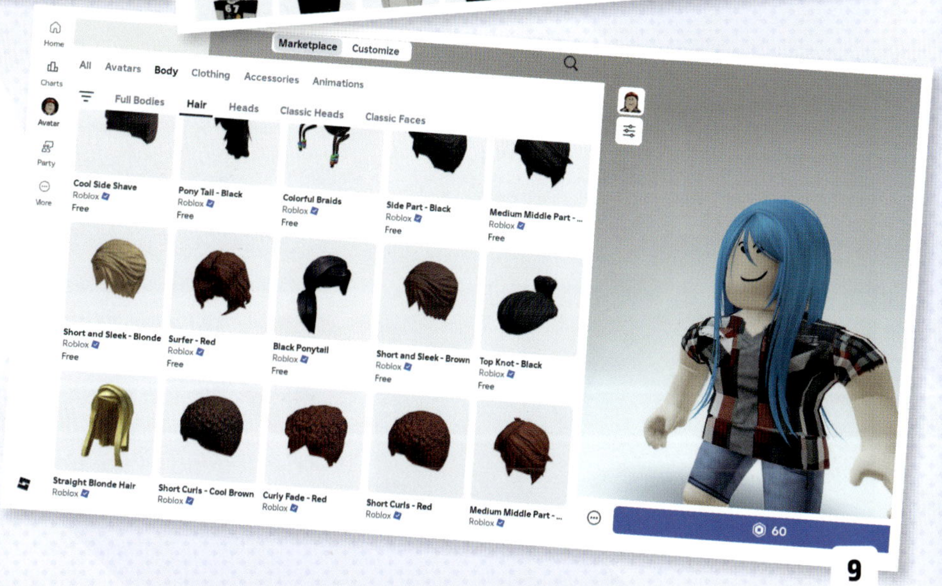

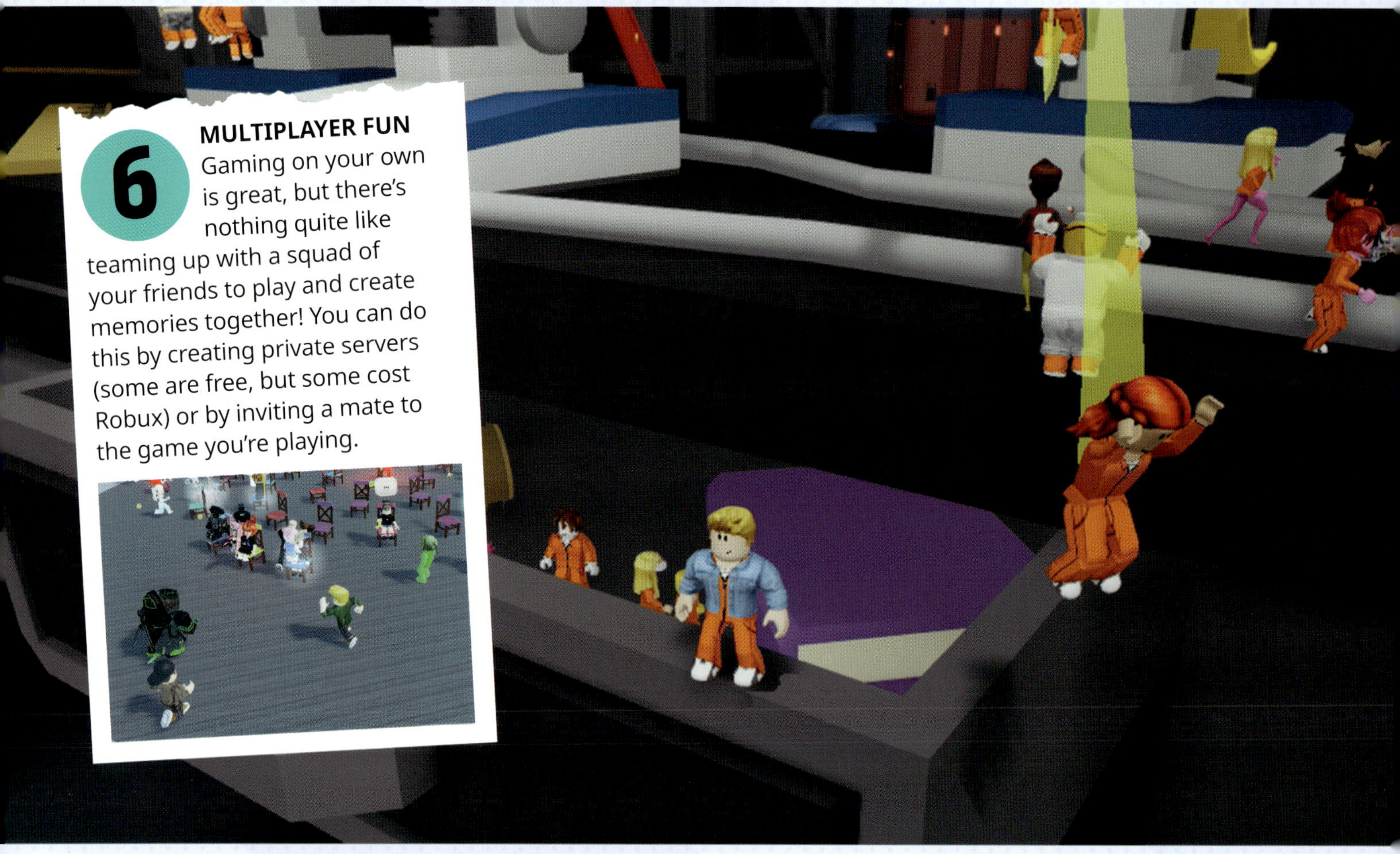

6 MULTIPLAYER FUN

Gaming on your own is great, but there's nothing quite like teaming up with a squad of your friends to play and create memories together! You can do this by creating private servers (some are free, but some cost Robux) or by inviting a mate to the game you're playing.

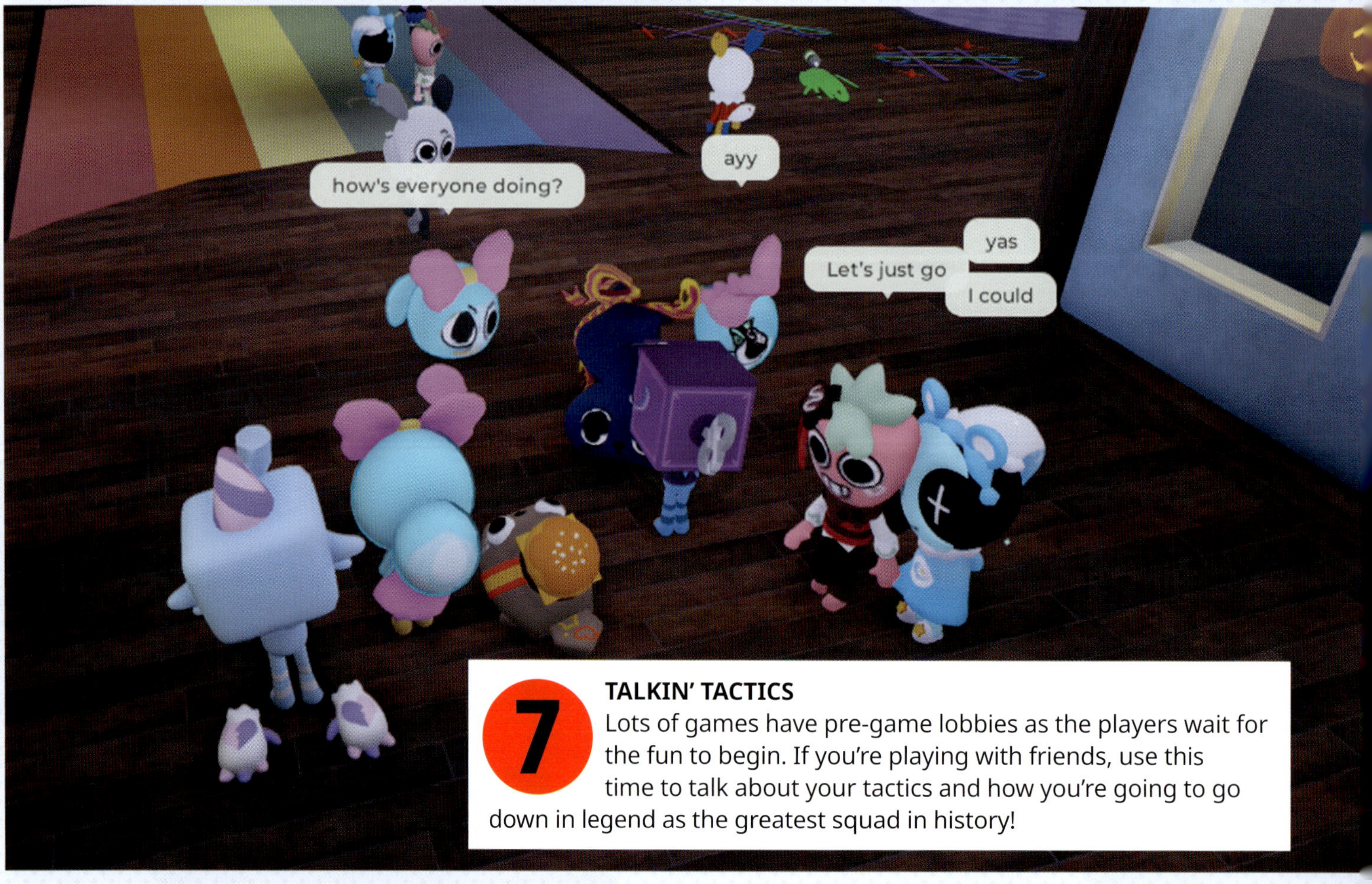

7 TALKIN' TACTICS

Lots of games have pre-game lobbies as the players wait for the fun to begin. If you're playing with friends, use this time to talk about your tactics and how you're going to go down in legend as the greatest squad in history!

8

COOL CUSTOMISATION

You can get your hands on loads of customisation at the Roblox Catalogue Marketplace, but there are some items that can only be earned by making progress in your favourite games. The more you play, the more you'll unlock! From in-game items to super powers and exclusive pets, you'll be rewarded for your dedication to a game!

ROBLOX ROYALTY

The best part about Roblox is that there are always amazing games (both new and old) to play! Let's celebrate some of the best award-winning experiences that have been making waves in the community.

OVER 25 BILLION VISITS

AWESOME ADVENTURE

Every Roblox experience is an adventure in its own way, but **99 Nights in the Forest** is an extreme adventure game! It was even voted the Best Adventure Experience! Players must survive in a forest by starting a fire, building a base, completing awesome challenges and defending themselves from the dark creatures of the wilderness!

ICONIC GAMES

Some games really stand the test of time, and **Brookhaven RP** is a favourite amongst fans. It won the award for best Roleplay & Avatar Simulator Experience and celebrated being the most-visited experience in Roblox history. If you haven't jumped in and created your own Brookhaven life, there's no better time than now to check it out!

OVER 78 BILLION VISITS

ALL-OUT SPORT

Sports games are becoming more and more popular amongst players, and **Basketball: Zero** took the gold medal for Best Sports Experience at the Roblox Awards. Players can't get enough of its fast-paced 5v5 basketball games, where the characters are all inspired by anime and can be buffed with amazing new styles, abilities and loot boxes to raid!

OVER 940 MILLION VISITS

TIME FOR A SCARE

Have you got a favourite horror game? They're still one of the most popular experiences, and players love the jump scares and gory situations! **Field Trip Z** is an epic horror story that sees a school trip disrupted by a zombie apocalypse. Typical! It's a rare choice-driven game, meaning your actions and decisions will change the way the game goes!

OVER 1.2 BILLION VISITS

RELISH IN ROLE-PLAY

Grow a Garden has been making headlines around the gaming world! It won five Roblox Awards, including Best Simulation, the People's Choice and the Builderman Award of Excellence! Check it out and enjoy the cute vibes of growing crops and creating a wonderful outside space of your own.

OVER 34 BILLION VISITS

BRAIN BUSTERS

In **Steal a Brainrot**, your goal is to build wealth by collecting rare brainrots! You can also rob them off other players, who can steal yours in return, so you need to build a safe and secure base. This hilariously random game was rewarded for its unique fun as it won the Best Creative Direction prize at the Roblox Awards. Quick, go and check your brainrots!

OVER 58 BILLION VISITS

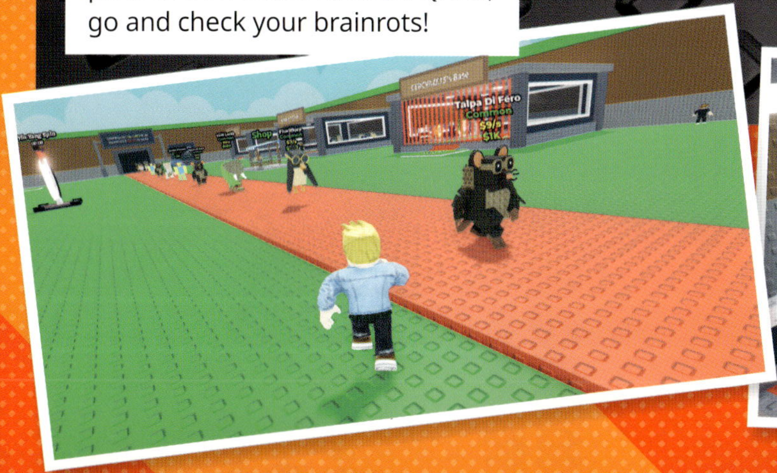

RISING STARS

We get it ... It can be difficult to find your next favourite game, so let us do the hard work for you! We've left no stone unturned in our search for the greatest up-and-coming games. Check out these hidden gems!

FIND THE PIZZA

You've never met a pizza as cheeky as Rasmus. This cheesy slice of deception just won't stay in its pan, and loves nothing more than hiding. Your task is to explore and find Rasmus across 50 different stages. These levels range from basic spotting to hardcore hide and seeking with tricky obstacles. There won't be just one slice to find during each round, so keep your eyes peeled for plenty of pizza!

BETTER FOOD?

Welcome to the tastiest multiplayer arena in town, and get ready for some tantalizing battles! As two different meals are shown on either side of the room (from mouth-watering roast dinners to delicious cakes), the other players vanish and you'll need to vote for your favourite food in secret. Once a countdown finishes, you'll see who else voted with you ... or against you! Then the winning food is decided by a big battle with funny weapons!

QUEST FOR THE LOST TV REMOTE

There's no panic like losing your TV remote, and this cartoon classic take you on a journey to find it ... through an extraordinary house. As you work your way through the many rooms, you'll meet mysterious objects, characters and find fun puzzles to solve. There are three chapters so far, so get ready for this story to get bigger as you solve its secrets!

WORDS OF POWER

Knowledge is truly power in this role-play game. You start by collecting exciting new words that supercharge your abilities. You must then progress through mystical worlds, whilst battling cool creatures. There are four realms and over one million battle combos to experiment with, so no two games are ever the same. You can play with your friends using fun items, like lucky clovers and powerful telescopes!

Garage Tuner

RATE MY CAR

This slick competition game is all about making cars look cool. Each round has a random theme, which can be anything from colour schemes to unique features, and you must race against the clock to create your custom ride. Pick new lights, bumpers, wings and rims, and then show it off for other players to rate. So, do you think you can win this eng-ineous competition?

UNTITLED TAG GAME

The chase is on in as you enjoy the fun of tag mixed with the thrill of parkour. Whether you're the hunter or the hunted, you can use controls to run, jump, vault, climb and scream your way to victory. Can you outwit and outmanoeuvre all of the other players to crown yourself the glorious winner of every round? There are loads of different levels and you'll need to master them all to move to the top of the leaderboard!

Try this:

Other players will guess you're the Tagger if you act sus. Try tricking them into thinking you're innocent, then pounce when they least suspect!

SURVIVAL MEGA MISSIONS

Ready for a chaotic challenge? It's time to pit your wits against forces of nature, creepy entities and tumbling towers in Roblox's greatest survival experiences. Can you make it to the very end still standing?

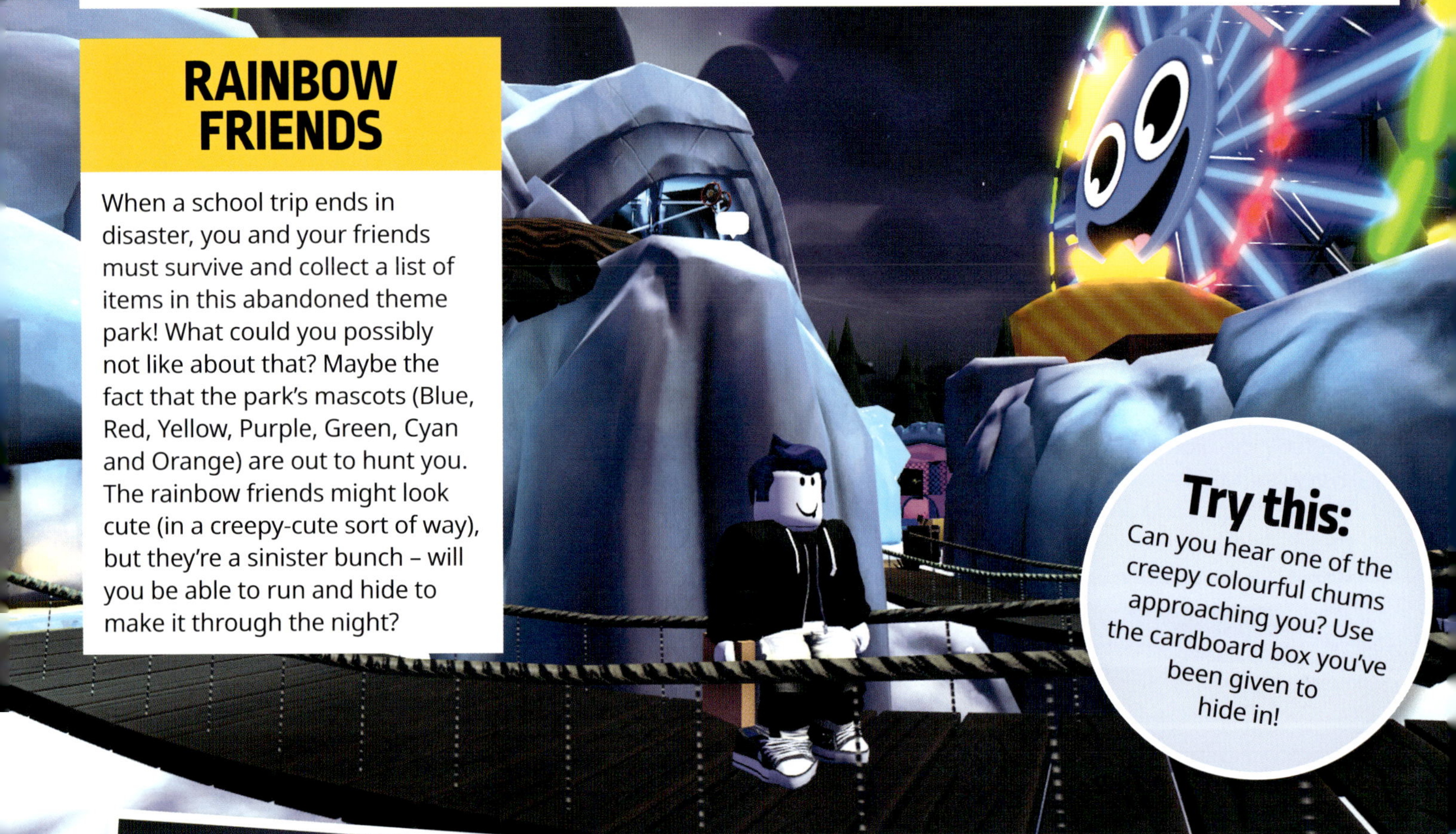

RAINBOW FRIENDS

When a school trip ends in disaster, you and your friends must survive and collect a list of items in this abandoned theme park! What could you possibly not like about that? Maybe the fact that the park's mascots (Blue, Red, Yellow, Purple, Green, Cyan and Orange) are out to hunt you. The rainbow friends might look cute (in a creepy-cute sort of way), but they're a sinister bunch – will you be able to run and hide to make it through the night?

Try this:
Can you hear one of the creepy colourful chums approaching you? Use the cardboard box you've been given to hide in!

SOMETHING EVIL WILL HAPPEN

Get ready! This game features an exciting new disaster every round, and your goal is to survive. You can do this by running, jumping and hiding. From brutal blizzards to frightening laser rain showers, you'll need to work with your team to stand any chance of making it to the next round. You can upgrade your powers with lots of cool status effects, such as Adrenaline which increases your sprinting speed. It's a frantic game, but so much fun!

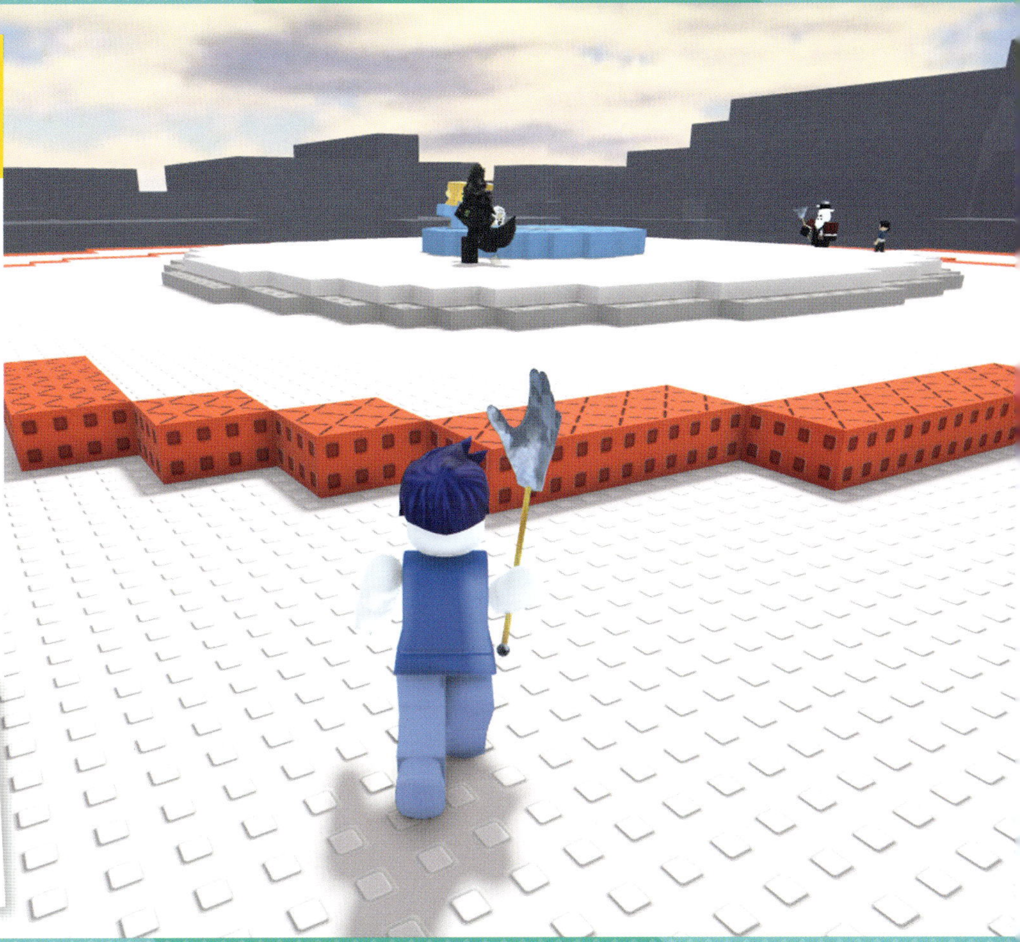

DESTROY THE TOWER

In this game you have to ... well, destroy the tower! There's one Thrower and the rest are Players. The Players must run around and avoid getting hit, and Throwers must throw items to destroy both the tower and the players. What items, you ask? Have you ever thrown a car at a building? This is one of the most satisfying experiences on Roblox! Don't stop until every single block has been broken, by any means necessary.

GIANT SURVIVAL!

Wowee! Look at the size of that giant. Imagine the poor players trying to defeat it ... which is exactly what you must to do in this game of humongous fun! As the giants get stronger and gain unique new powers, you'll need to level-up your weapons and choose the perfect loadout and tactical approach to stand a chance of survival!

BEDWARS

It's time to protect yourself, and, more importantly, your bed in this hilarious game. You'll also need to work with your team to upgrade your abilities and find a way to enemy islands. Once there, destroy any enemy beds you can get your battle claws on, but don't lose sight of your own ... the enemy will be attacking them! But remember, stay alert and stay awake – this is no snooze-fest!

Best of the rest

Even more survival showdowns!

BUILD A BOAT FOR TREASURE

Build your own boat and set off in search of valuable loot and precious treasure. You'll have to be creative with your builds and survive the onslaught of obstacles. Land ahoy!

BOOGA BOOGA

This epic island-roaming game mixes travel, survival and building! Explore mysterious islands and create tribes to populate and protect your land ... then raid opposing tribes!

SHARK BITE

There's something in the water! Play as survivors and try to escape a killer shark that's on the hunt for its next meal ... which happens to be your boat! You can even play as the shark.

TOP TIPS

Make survival easier!

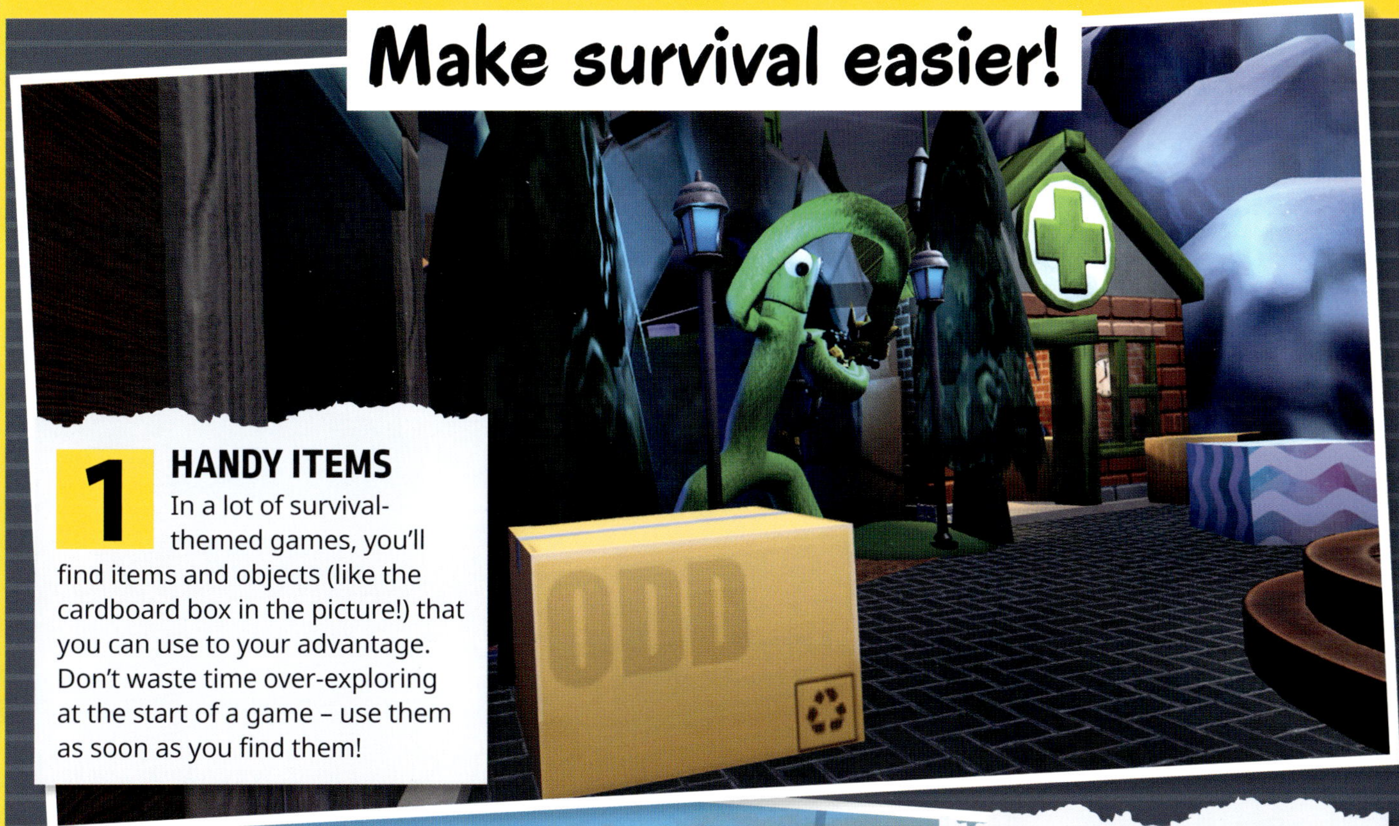

1 HANDY ITEMS

In a lot of survival-themed games, you'll find items and objects (like the cardboard box in the picture!) that you can use to your advantage. Don't waste time over-exploring at the start of a game – use them as soon as you find them!

2 GO EXPLORE

Once it's safe, try to get to know the level you're on (like the player is doing in the picture, venturing outside of the farmhouse). You might discover useful items or locations that'll help you later on when the trouble arrives. But always remember the fastest route back to somewhere safe!

3 AN AIM GAME

In many survival games, you can use weapons, items and special powers to defeat enemies and even large structures (like these tall towers in the picture). Practise using the weapons and tools to get the perfect launch and aim. Once you've mastered in-game tools, you'll be well on your way to being a total master of survival!

YOUR ROBLOX EMPIRE

It's time to get to work, start your own business and build an empire! There are so many tycoon games on Roblox to choose from, and each one gives you the chance to be the best boss in town!

EGG EMPIRE

In this egg-citing game, you need to build your very own farm, then spawn chickens and care for them as they lay their eggs. You can then sell eggs to pay for upgrades to your farm (such as chicken houses and vehicles), unlock prestige mechanics and hire workers to help you. You can also research new egg tiers, from Galaxy eggs and Yeti eggs, to the incredible Overlord egg! Wow!

MEGA BUTTERFLY TYCOON

Love tycoon games but want to build your own empire and a slower (and cosier) pace? Try Mega Butterfly Tycoon! Start with a small plot of land and earn money to expand your collection of butterflies and create new structures, such as greenhouses and butterfly houses! You can even build them special features to flutter around, like fountains and picnic areas!

TREE MANSION TYCOON!

Everyone dreams of building their own treehouse, and this game will bring your wildest ideas to life! Starting with a simple patch of land, you must earn money to build up into the sky. The more you earn, the more you can gradually add cool bling to yours, with neon lights, gaming rooms and loads more. Don't forget to visit other players' treehouses to admire them and find inspiration!

MEGA MANSION TYCOON

If luxury houses and cars is what you're after, then look no further than Mega Mansion Tycoon. Earn money to upgrade both your lavish mansion and your fleet of super cars, which you can take to the streets and race against other players. Become successful enough to buy a boat or helicopter and you'll be able to explore secret offshore locations!

RESTAURANT TYCOON 2

It's time to rise to the top of the culinary world, as you build, design and run your very own restaurant. In this chaotic, cusine challenge, you get to choose your restaurant design, pick the menu and master your equipment. But make sure you are super-speedy, as you'll need to keep your customers happy to turn a profit. The happier they are, the more they'll tip you! You can then expand your operation with a additions like a Drive-thru. Tasty!

Best of the rest

Time for more tycoon games?

LUMBER TYCOON 2

Explore the world of Lumberland to harvest and sell wood from trees. Use your profits to build a dream home in the wilderness!

THEME PARK TYCOON 2

Build, manage, customise and ride in this epic tycoon game. Keep your guests happy and you could get a five star rating. Win!

ZOMBIE MERGE TYCOON

In this gruesome take on a tycoon game, you run a base where you must breed zombies and defend your base from ... more zombies!

TOP TIPS

Be the best in business!

1 SIMPLE ROOTS

Rome wasn't built in a day – and your empire will take some time. Start small and focus on saving up your money instead of spending it all at once. Before long, you'll be ready to expand beyond your wildest dreams. Then one day, you'll be able to afford something as cool as this massive treehouse in the picture!

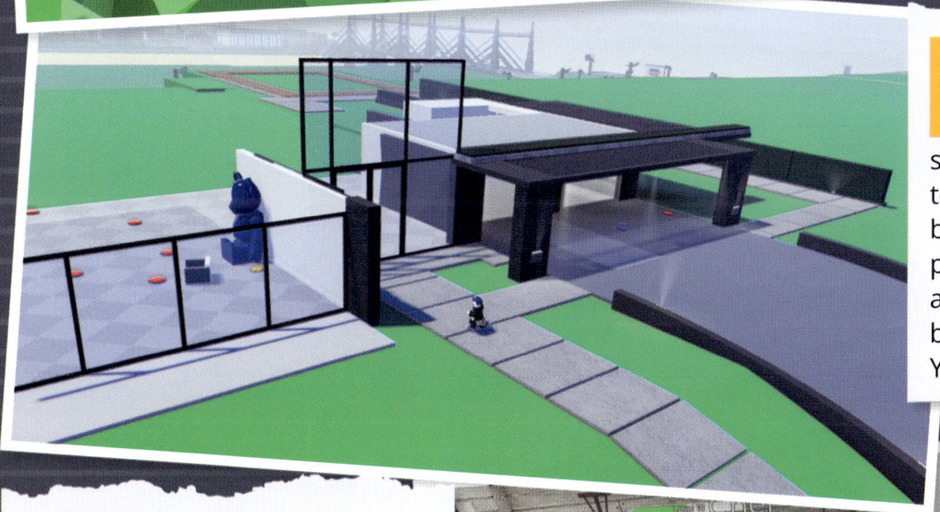

2 LUXURY LIFE

Once you've put aside a bit of cash, you'll want to start upgrading your restaurant to make the big bucks. Make your business even more efficient by purchasing bigger extensions, adding fancy equipment and buying some cute decorations. Your customers will love it!

3 HAPPY HELPERS

When you first start out, you'll need to lead by example and put the work in yourself. But as soon as you can, focus on hiring workers. This way, you can take a step back and focus on bigger picture problems. Maybe you could develop a new menu or unlock more pets. It's up to you!

CUTE AND COSY ADVENTURES

Sometimes we all want to relax and enjoy some cute experiences that makes us feel calm and cosy! These games do all of that and more, from pet collecting skims to adorble tycoon experiences. Aaaaand relax!

TOWER OF COFFEE

If you find obby games a bit too manic, then this cosy coffee course is for you. Roblox fans love how relaxing this game is, and we can't blame them. Each obby is inside a tower named after a different type of coffee drink, from caramel latte to pink matcha latte! That said, some of the harder towers are a serious challenge that only a few talented coffee connoisseurs can conquer!

Try this:
There's even an adorable dress up area for you to try on cute accessories, from teddy bear hats to adorable bows. What will you try first?

GROW A GARDEN

In the first year of its release, this game received over 34 billion visits and its popularity is still, well, growing! In this game, you must create a cosy garden that is peaceful and productive, so you can harvest rare crops and spend your earnings at the seed and gear shops. If that wasn't enough, you can hatch pets from special eggs – and they'll help make your garden even better!

COLLECT ALL PETS!

As the name suggests, this game sets you on a mission to collect many magical pets. How much time do you have? Because there are over 240 pets to hunt for! Amazingly, you can fuse pets together to make more powerful versions – with the shiny variants being the most sought after pets in the game!

CAKE OFF!

Race against the clock in this speedy baking extravaganza! Every round has a different theme, and your task is to impress the judges with your creativity. You can customise your bake in lots of different ways, like different tiers, mad icing, unique decorations and unexpected fillings and flavours. You also get to vote on other players' cakes – so try and be sweet to them!

BACKPACK ADVENTURE: FIND THE ANIMALS

What's more cosy than a long nature walk, spotting adorable animals along the way? Grab your camera and document every animal you can, with over 60 furry creatures to discover across a world of unique biomes! Find them all and you'll be rewarded with items, like the Backpack Explorer Bald Eagle Wings. Neat!

PET SIMULATOR 99!

This is the ultimate pet collecting game, and it's one of the largest experiences in all of Roblox! There are over 2,000 unique pets to collect, and they vary in rarity from basic to exclusive variants. There are also titanic pets – which, you guessed it – are huge! Your pets will help you earn credits by breaking coins, crates and chests. You can even trade pets, if you can bear to part with them!

Try this:

Focus on unlocking new areas as soon as you can, as they will offer bigger chests and crates! The bigger the loot, the more fun you'll uncover.

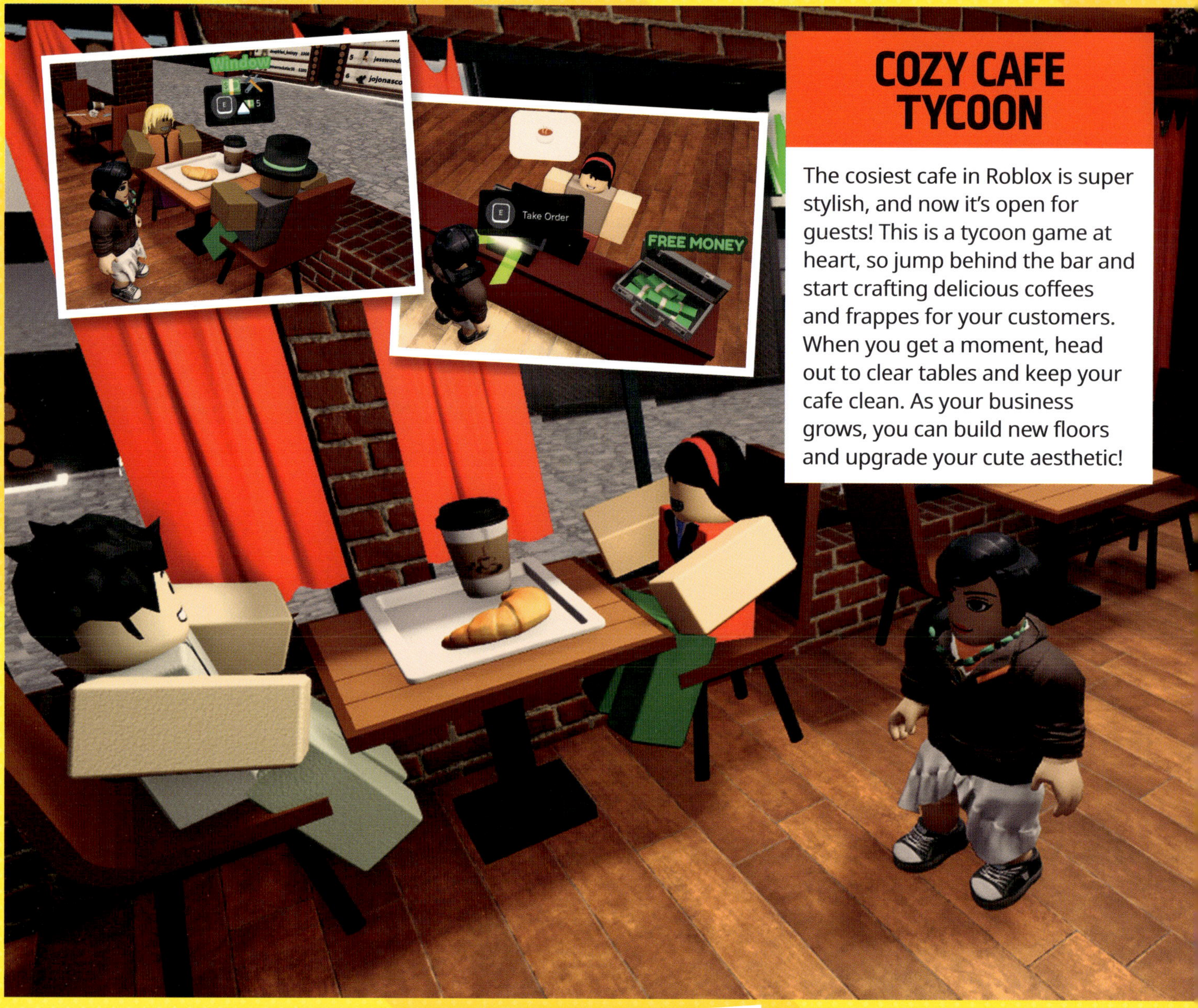

COZY CAFE TYCOON

The cosiest cafe in Roblox is super stylish, and now it's open for guests! This is a tycoon game at heart, so jump behind the bar and start crafting delicious coffees and frappes for your customers. When you get a moment, head out to clear tables and keep your cafe clean. As your business grows, you can build new floors and upgrade your cute aesthetic!

Best of the rest

Keep it cosy for longer with these!

WELCOME TO BLOXBURG

The original and (perhaps the best!) simulation sees you build, work and play. Buy a mansion, chat with pals and more!

TREASURE HUNT SIMULATOR

Look away if you don't like having sand between your toes! Search for treasure to upgrade tools, your backpack and more.

PICNICS N PLUSHIES

The ultimate cosy game to snuggle up with! Collect boxes hidden around the map to unlock money and plushies.

TOP TIPS

How to be a cosy legend!

1 TAKE YOUR TIME

There's no need to rush about trying to complete quests in these games! Why not put on your favourite playlist and just enjoy slow tasks like unlocking eggs, enjoying the scenery and more.

2 GRIND AND GAIN

Cute games like Grow A Garden take time to achieve maximum cosiness. The more you play, the more you will unlock! Engage with NPCs (non-player characters), plant your crops, sell your items and participate in special events!

3 CUSTOM COOL

You can make all of these games even sweeter with their options and unlockables. There's nothing better than dressing your avatar up in the best accessories before you take part in some wholesome activities. Feeling cosy is half the fun of going into these games!

FAST FAVOURITES

There are loads of Roblox experiences that feature obstacle courses packed with epic twists and turns! They're known as obby games, and it's a true test to walk, run, jump and hop through. Just don't fall to pieces!

ESCAPE THE CARNIVAL OF TERROR OBBY!

Being locked inside an abandoned carnival by an evil clown doesn't sound like much fun, but this game brings so many puzzles, traps and obstacles that it's frighteningly good fun! The aim is to escape, and you'll need to survive the rides and progress through each area to beat it. It's all made harder by the fact that the clown will try to scare you ... by attacking you when you least expect it!

Try this:

Use the 'double jump' technique to overcome some of the game's larger drop sections. Without it, you'll fall before getting very far!

CARRY A FISH

In an amazing take on a classic obby, this two-player game sees one player take on the role of the fisher ... and the other player as the fish! The fisher must tackle increasingly difficult maps, whilst carrying the fish as they swing around on the end of a fishing rod. Sound easy? It isn't! Obby courses are twice as difficult when one of you is swinging and taking damage at every turn!

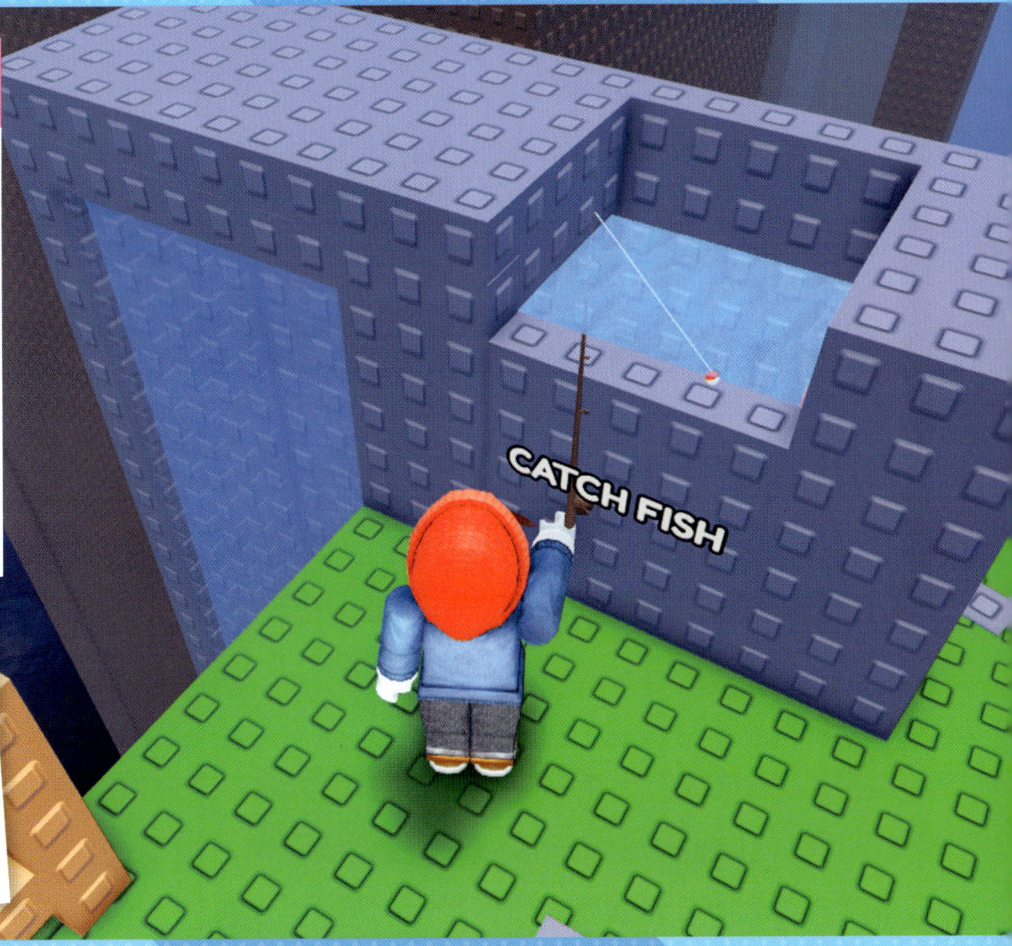

THE DROPPER

Unlike many obby experiences, in this game you actually need to fall to reach the finish – but it isn't as easy as simply jumping off! As you fall, different obstacles and items will suddenly appear to block your way, so you'll need to scan the area ahead as you drop. There's been loads of updates to this classic game and with over 130 different levels, there's always a new reason to drop in!

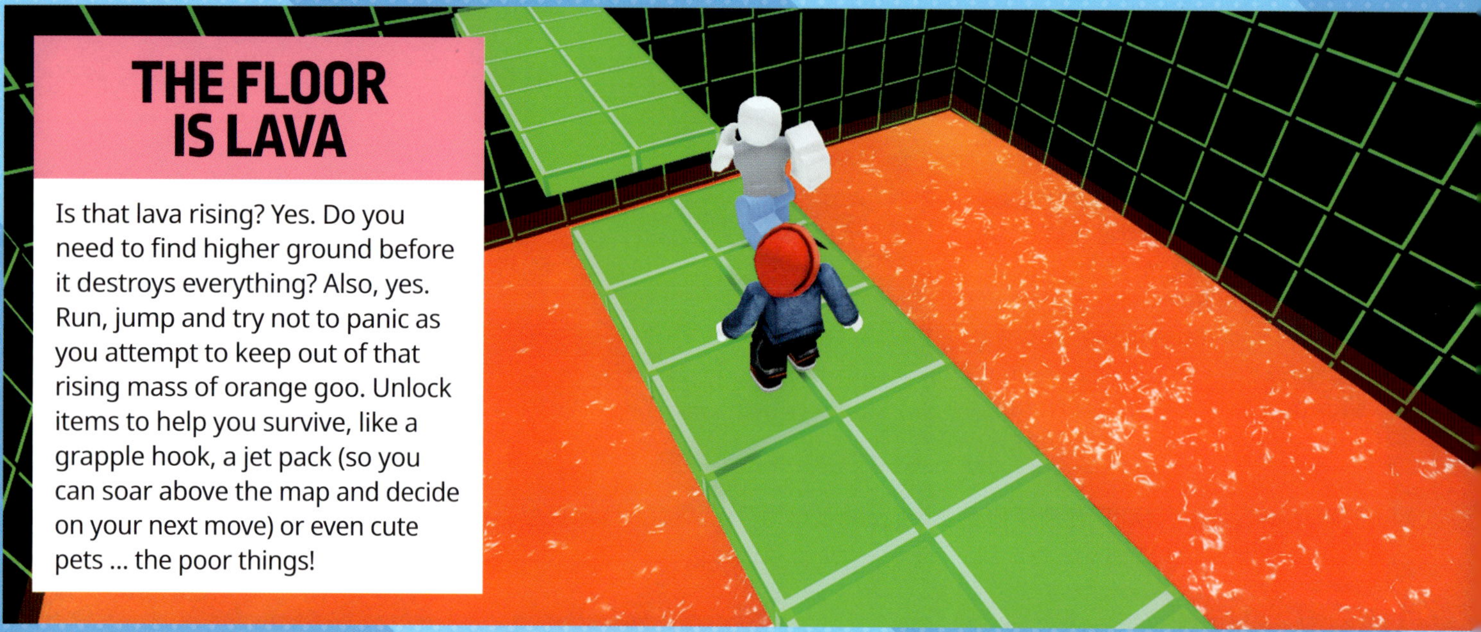

THE FLOOR IS LAVA

Is that lava rising? Yes. Do you need to find higher ground before it destroys everything? Also, yes. Run, jump and try not to panic as you attempt to keep out of that rising mass of orange goo. Unlock items to help you survive, like a grapple hook, a jet pack (so you can soar above the map and decide on your next move) or even cute pets ... the poor things!

BIKE OF HELL

This obby takes place entirely in the sky, which is exciting until you realise you have to ride a bike across the obstacles. Pedal as fast as you can over the airborne hurdles, and try to beat other players to the finish. If that wasn't scary enough, you can jump to make your bike go faster! Races last over six minutes and there are loads of different courses to try and master.

Best of the rest

Need more obby games? Jump into these!

MEGA EASY OBBY

Despite its name, this game is seriously tricky! With over 800 levels, you'll have hours of fun on bonkers courses. Will you find it mega easy by the time you've completed it?

PARKOUR RUN!

The courses on this speedrun randomly generate as you move, so you never know what's next. Use items to slow down players and hope the course doesn't generate anything to stop you!

MEGA FUN OBBY

Is this obby fun? You bet it is! This is one of Roblox's longest obstacle games and can be played alone or with friends and family. There are over 2,800 stages and new levels are always added!

TOP TIPS

To conquer any obby!

1 BALANCING ACT

To beat almost every obby game, you'll need to move carefully and master the art of balancing. Start by moving slowly to get a feel for the controls, then build up your pace until you're speeding along!

2 THINK TWICE

When you can see the course ahead of you, take a moment to study its twists, turns and traps. If you've got a plan, you will always find it easier to make it to the end of the course without failing.

3 TEAMWORK

Many obbies can be played alone, but lots of them can be played in a team. If you're part of a squad, work together to navigate the more difficult sections. If someone tries something and falls to their doom ... maybe try something different when it's you're turn!

MULTIPLAYER MASTERCLASS

Playing on your own will always be fun, but playing with friends is pure jokes! There's nothing more entertaining than working together to beat bosses, dominate the game and create laughs for days!

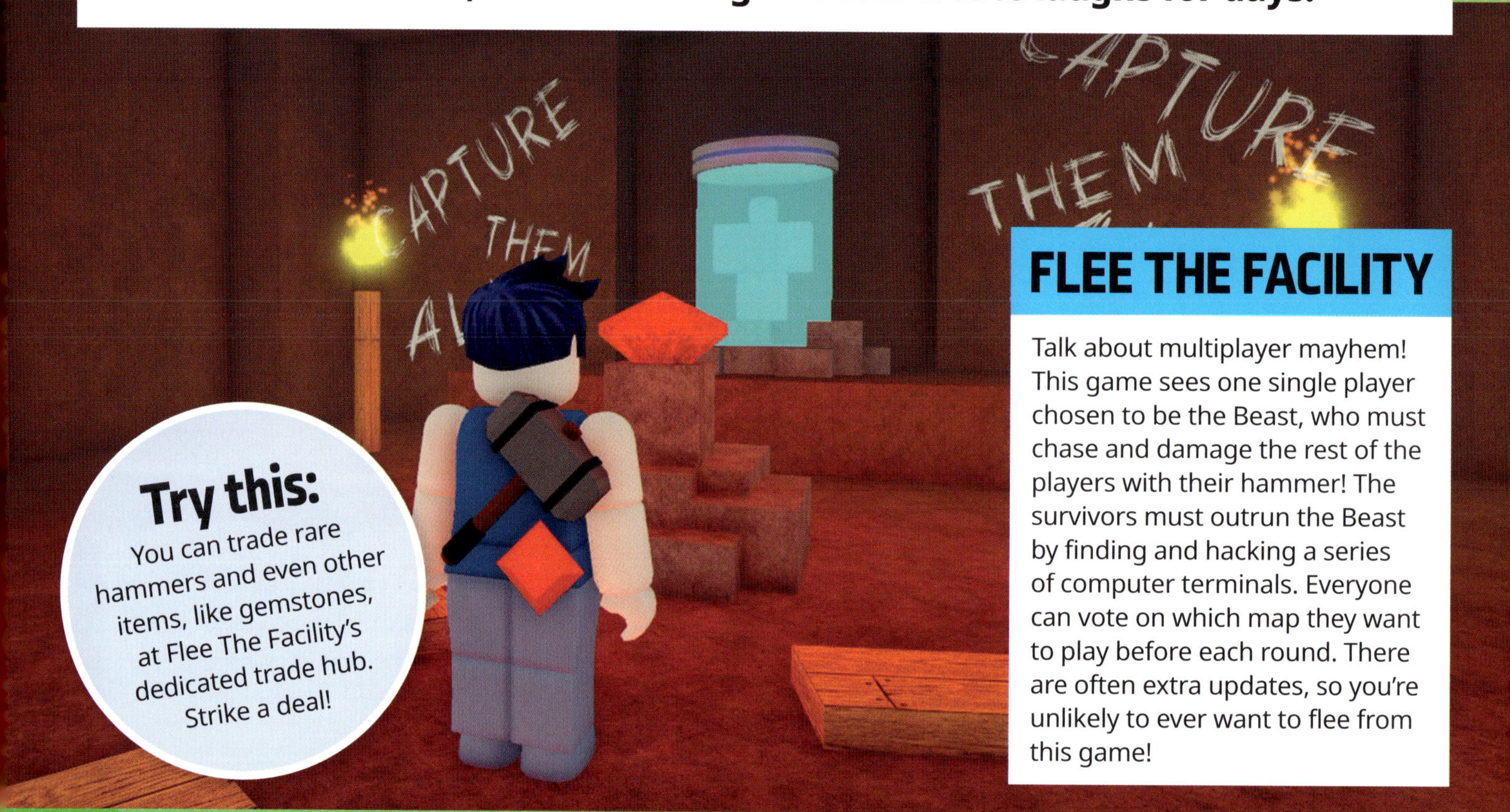

Try this:

You can trade rare hammers and even other items, like gemstones, at Flee The Facility's dedicated trade hub. Strike a deal!

FLEE THE FACILITY

Talk about multiplayer mayhem! This game sees one single player chosen to be the Beast, who must chase and damage the rest of the players with their hammer! The survivors must outrun the Beast by finding and hacking a series of computer terminals. Everyone can vote on which map they want to play before each round. There are often extra updates, so you're unlikely to ever want to flee from this game!

RIVALS

This ridiculously fast-paced, first-person shooter is all about the player-vs-player action! Up to 10 gamers take part at any one time, and they have over 40 different weapons to pick from. It uses a skill-based matchmaking system, so you'll always be put against players with similar skills to you – the perfect way to get better. Think fast and fire even faster!

BUILD AN ISLAND

It's time to develop your very own tropical paradise! First, gather wood and rocks to start building. Then you can start trading with Merchant Mike for seeds to grow crops. You can team up with your friends to build co-op islands that up to seven of you can work on! You can visit other people's islands to gain ideas and inspiration on what to do next on yours! Will island life suit you?

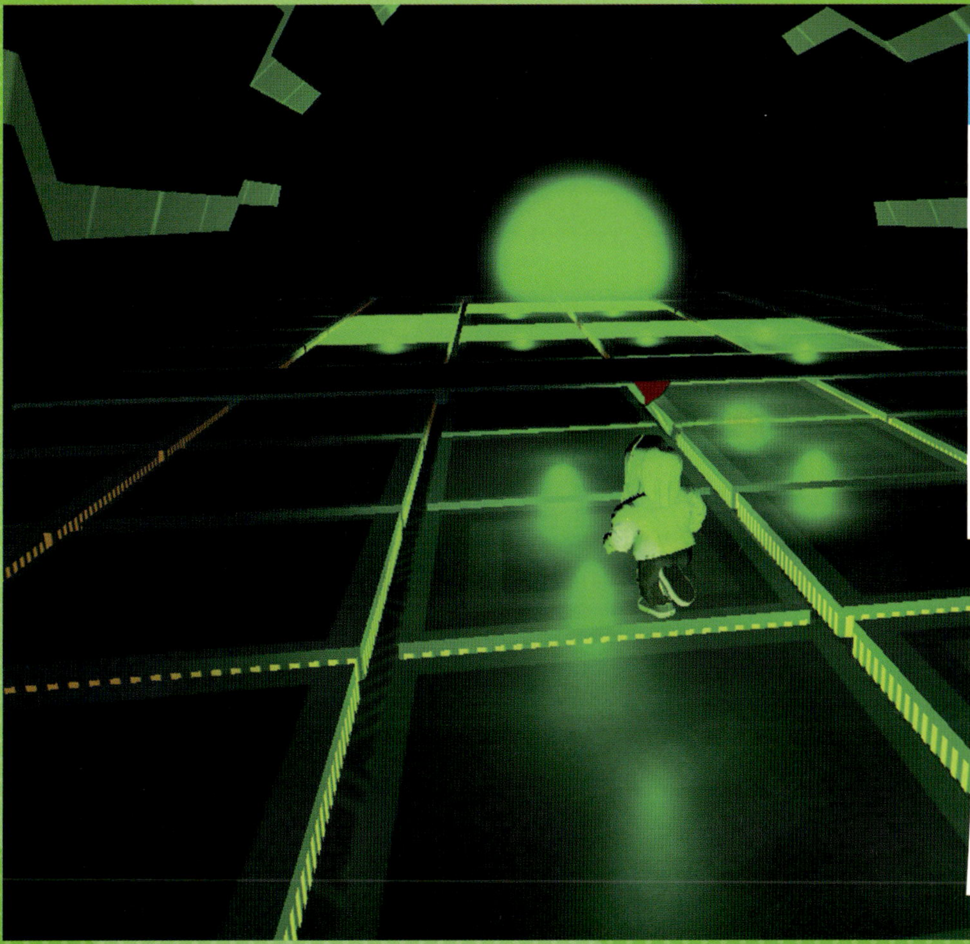

ROBLOX PARTY!

Grab your mates and get ready to party, as this experience brings the fun of board games to your gaming sessions! Players take it in turns to roll digital dice to move around the board. You can take part in fun mini-games, like dodgeball, to win rounds and fill their progress bar with crowns. You can gather up to 10 friends for this party. Who will win?

TOGETHER (PARTY GAME)

This game got it's name from the amount of collaboration needed to complete it! You'll need to work with your mates to take on obbies that have some seriously challenging obstacles. They're set in loads of cool locations, from a volcano alley to a deep ocean, and these get more and more difficult the further you get. You can play with as few as two players, or more for extra chaos!

HIDE AND SEEK EXTREME

The roles are decided and your countdown begins ... are you ready? The hiders have 60 seconds to find somewhere to hide before It (the seeker) is set loose! Can It find all of the players before they run out of time? The player who is It can even use special abilities to help them, like placing glue puddles! Will ANY hiders survive to the end?

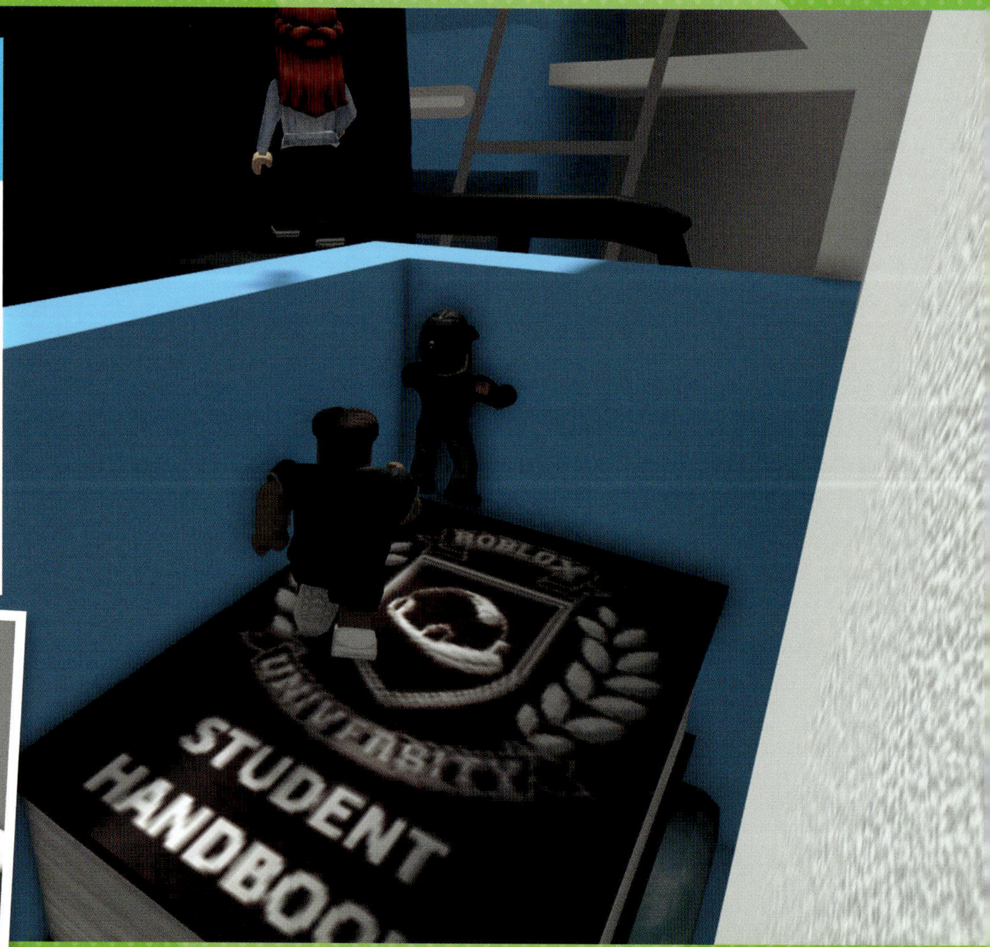

SPEED DRAW!

Competitive games are rarely as fun and creative as this! Players are given a new theme at the start of each round and must then create a piece of digital artwork using the tools provided. Sound easy? Ha, we know it doesn't! At the end of each round, everyone will vote on each other's art before a podium ceremony for the winners!

SLAP BATTLES

If you haven't played this game before, where have you been hiding?! Players take it in turns to slap each other, using one of 240 special gloves. There's a battle royale mode that features up to 30 players battling to be the last player standing! If that sounds too easy, try the tournaments using just a basic glove and a shrinking platform that'll send you hurtling into the abyss!

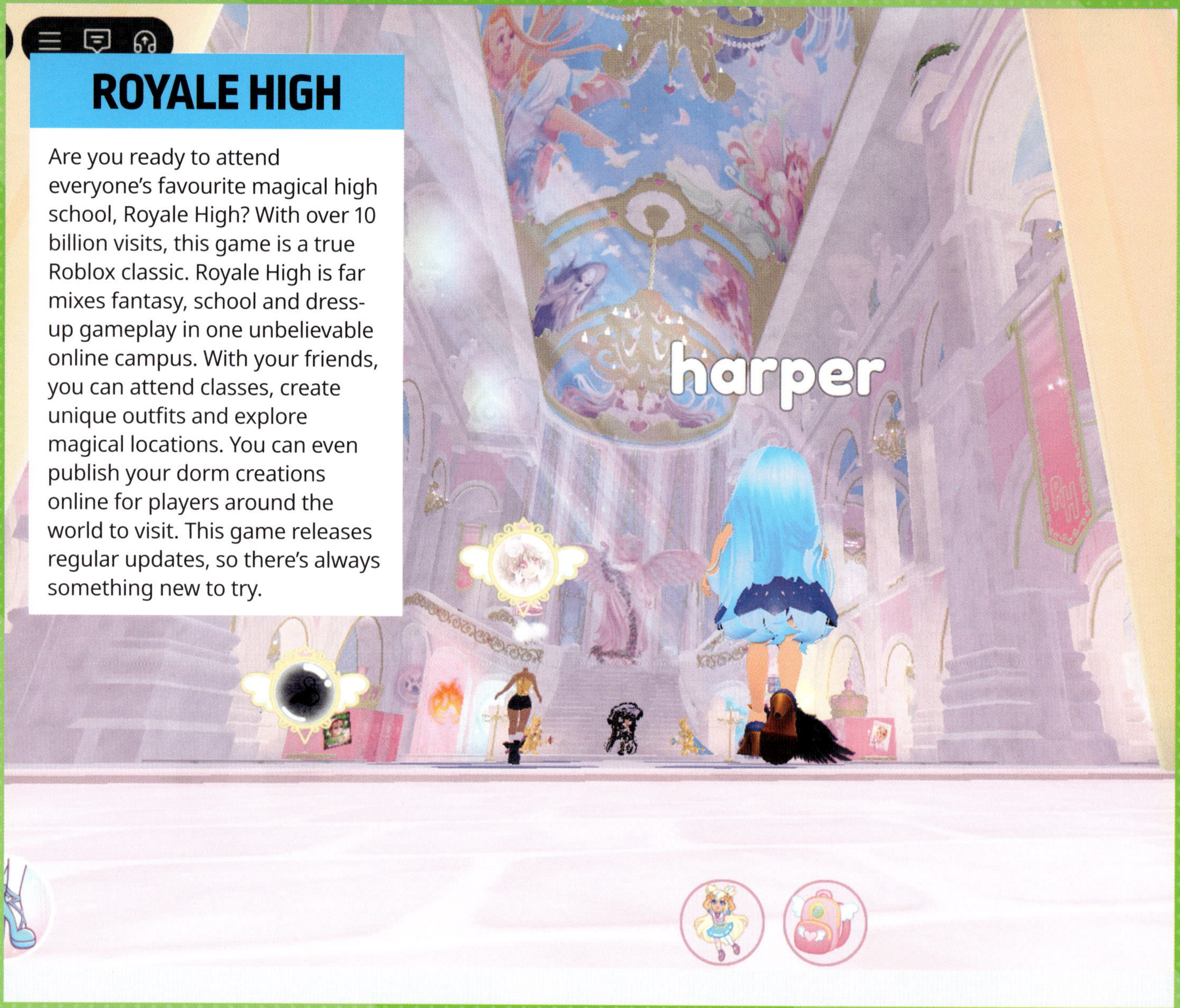

ROYALE HIGH

Are you ready to attend everyone's favourite magical high school, Royale High? With over 10 billion visits, this game is a true Roblox classic. Royale High is far mixes fantasy, school and dress-up gameplay in one unbelievable online campus. With your friends, you can attend classes, create unique outfits and explore magical locations. You can even publish your dorm creations online for players around the world to visit. This game releases regular updates, so there's always something new to try.

Best of the rest

Want more multiplayer mayhem?

BLOX FRUITS

Sail the seas and complete quests along the way. Plus battle players you encounter with the unique power of blox fruits, which you can collect on your travels!

WORK AT A PIZZA PLACE

Work has never been this much fun! Join other players working shifts at Builder Brothers Pizza, and earn money to fund new upgrades to your very own house!

TEAMWORK PUZZLES 2

Many obby games are solo experiences, but this one is all about working together. Team up in duos, trios or quads and see if you can conquer the courses!

TOP TIPS

To master multiplayer!

1 IT TAKES TWO

Multiplayer games are all about working as a team, and that means looking out for your pal. Is your mate exploring a spooky looking area and they look like they need back-up? Then face the doorway and keep an eye out for bosses and players coming in to attack – like in the image above!

2 CELEBRATE!

Remember to celebrate your achievements in Roblox! Have you just won a fast-paced game in Rivals, like these two players in the picture? Then strike a pose and celebrate with your pal.

3 PLAN ROLES

Everyone in your squad will have different strengths. In the lobby before every game, message each other so you all know what role you'll be best suited to. Perhaps you're great at obbies, like the green player in the picture? Then get the squad to follow your lead! Or perhaps you're great at puzzle solving, like the grey player in the image? Then stand further back to offer your mates some support!

FIVE FANTASY QUESTS

Longing for a new adventure? A fan of magical creatures? Then leave the real world behind and enter the mystical realms of other dimensions, as we bring you the greatest fantasy games of all time.

VESTERIA

Vesteria is full of fantasy fans, thanks to its enormous open world, amazing character evolution and different player classes to choose from. Take on the role of a warrior, a mage or a hunter and learn the basics about combat and quests. Then go on to level up your character by beating powerful bosses and completing thrilling missions throughout the world. The more you play, the more powerful you'll become!

Try this:

You'll begin the experience in Scruff's Farm and Mushtown. Try to master the basics here before leaving, or you'll be unprepared for the wider world!

ASTRO RENAISSANCE

Set in outer space, this fantastical sci-fi dress-up game is a really social experience. It's perfect for playing with friends, or making new allies as you experiment with cosmic customisations! Travel to different planets that have their own themes, and earn Moonstones by completing quests. You can also win tickets by taking on mini-games and exchange them for Moonstones!

DRAGON ADVENTURES

Ever wanted a pet dragon? Then this is the game for you! You'll embark on a magical and thrilling adventure, where you'll tame dragons and explore new worlds! You'll start by finding dragon eggs and raise them from cute babies to all-powerful beasts with their own elemental powers (fire, water or grass), which will shape the way you play. Just wait until you get to soar in the sky on your favourite pet dragon! Yes, you heard us right!

ELEMENTAL DUNGEONS

If you love combat with a fantastical twist, then this dungeon crawler game is the one for you! Explore the amazing maps and defeat brutal bosses to earn experience points and upgrade your elemental abilities. Once you level-up enough, you'll be able to unlock awakenings, which will grant you supreme boosts to your powers – but will you have what it takes to survive the dungeons and be the best?

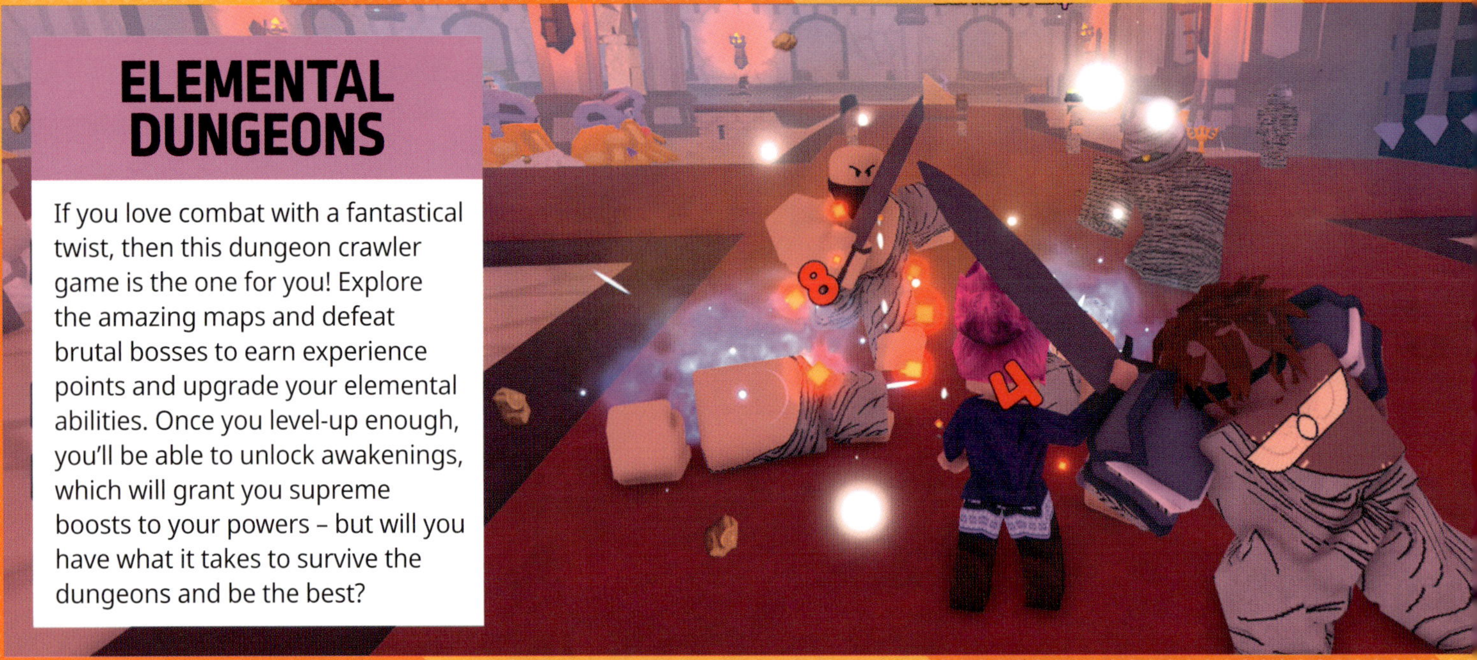

WORLD // ZERO ANIME RPG

Inspired by legendary anime, this massive multiplayer game is a fan-favourite in the Roblox community. When you start, you can pick to be one of three starter classes: Swordmaster, Arcane Mage and Defender. If you enjoy incredible landscapes, soothing music and tons of quests, then this is the game for you. There are also over 50 awesome pets to collect. Winner!

Best of the rest

Let the fantasy continue with these!

INFINITY RPG

Slay mobs and beat bosses to make your mark in this mega role-play game! If you earn enough gold, you might reach the incredible infinity status!

RPG SIMULATOR

The name of the game in RPG Simulator is to level-up your character as you battle through exciting zones, from the basic plains to an ancient jungle!

CREATURES OF SONARIA

Set in an enormous open-world, this game sees you play as a mysterious creature. Will you play as a cute little terror or a gigantic mega monster? You decide!

TOP TIPS

To complete the quests!

1 PET PATROL

Don't underestimate your pets! They aren't just cute mascots ... they can often be upgraded to have brilliant powers and abilities. Cute creatures like this little deer in the picture could be the difference between a win and a loss, or even just levelling up!

2 ENJOY IT

Exploring and enjoying fantasy worlds (like the cool carnival area with stalls and twinkly lights from Astro Renaissance within the picture) is one of the best parts about playing the games! Don't worry about racing through to progress in the game – just play at your own pace.

3 LOOK AROUND

The more you explore in fantasy games, the more cool secrets you'll uncover! But don't just go to crowded areas, head for concealed rooms and hidden areas (like this player has done in the quiet campfire area in the picture), as there could be loot and other helpful items.

SUPER SIMULATORS

Ah, simulators! They're a classic mash-up of lots of different genres, so there will definitely be one that is perfect for you. In these games, you can express yourself, hang out with friends, trade items, collect pets and more!

Try this:
If you hatch eggs and care for pets, this will add awesome multipliers to your powers. This part of the game is huge, as progression is key!

PILLOW FIGHTING SIMULATOR

Live a life of cushion combat by swinging to win more experience and gain strength. You can battle against other players or NPCs (non-playable characters) to earn upgrades, like mega new areas. Want to fight in the dreamland or the dojo? Or even get your hands on the dino or manface pillows? Keep on battling and they could be yours – and you'll be the envy of your mates!

LAUNDRY SIMULATOR

Whoever said doing laundry is a chore was seriously wrong! This game is all about making your laundromat become a success. Start by collecting laundry and placing it in your industrial washing machines, then earn gold by completing sets. You can upgrade your equipment to make your business the best in town!

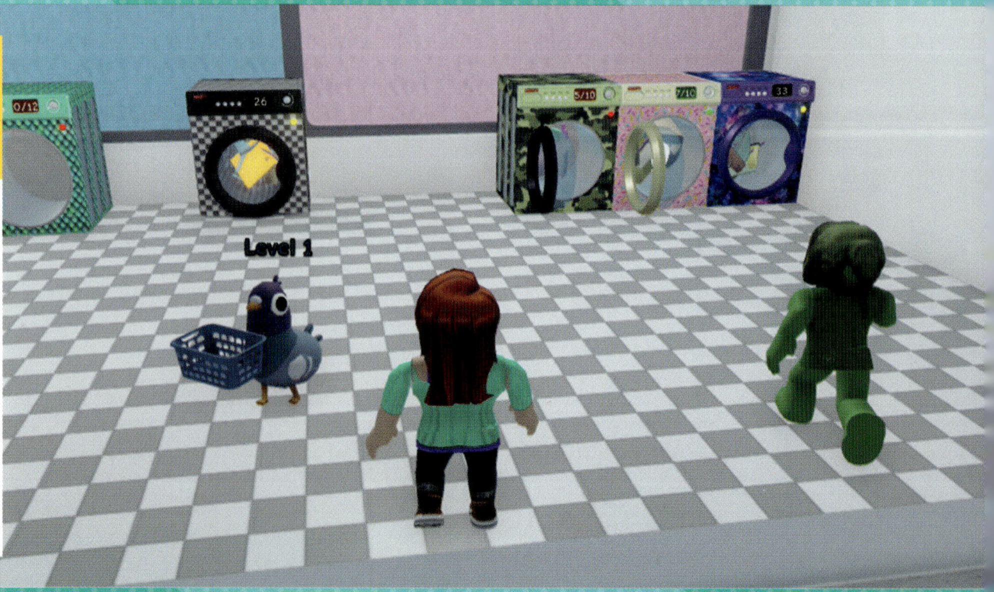

BEE SWARM SIMULATOR

Start your own swarm of bees and let them fly free to collect pollen and turn it into delicious honey! There are loads of special bees with their own characteristics, so who knows what they'll bring back after they float off into the different flower fields! Whilst they're busy, you can explore, and possibly meet some wild bears – they'll give you fun quests for special rewards. How friendly!

Try this:

The more honey you collect, the more fun you can have! You can use it to buy a bigger backpack and even more bee eggs. How sweet!

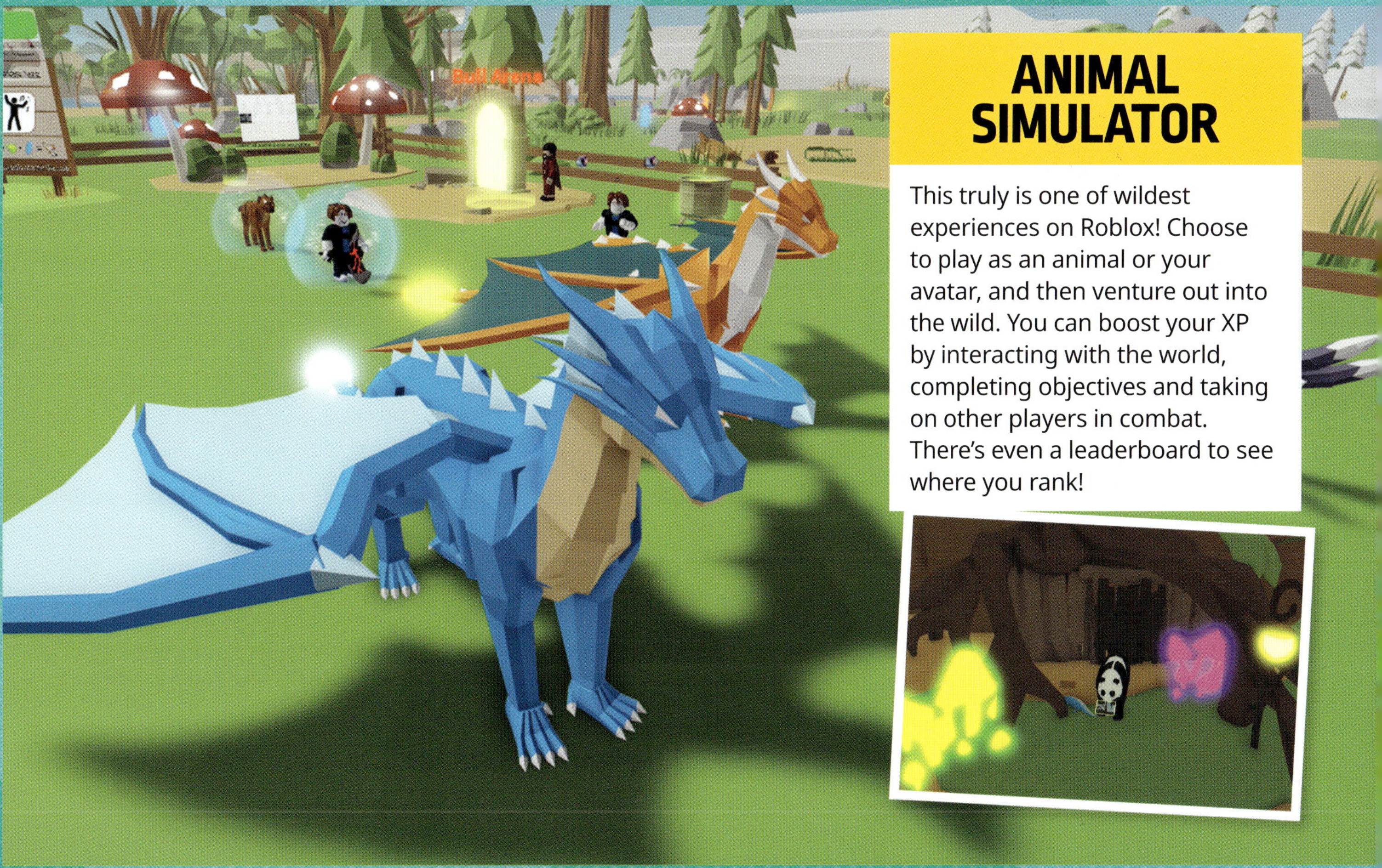

ANIMAL SIMULATOR

This truly is one of wildest experiences on Roblox! Choose to play as an animal or your avatar, and then venture out into the wild. You can boost your XP by interacting with the world, completing objectives and taking on other players in combat. There's even a leaderboard to see where you rank!

Try this:

Remember to cover all areas of the map and collect all of the coins. Your pets will smash open eggs, which will drop more coins – so never stop collecting!

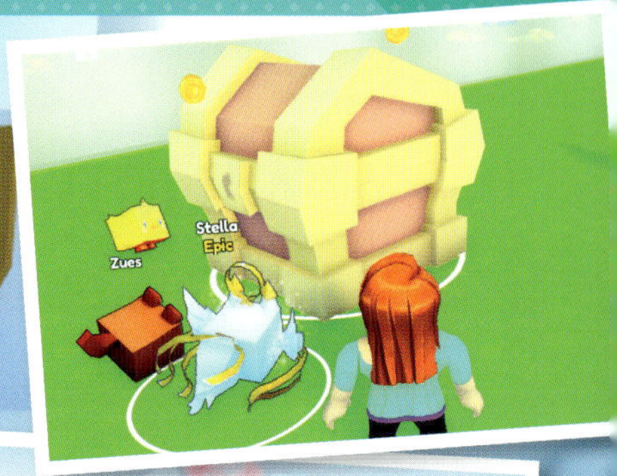

PET SIMULATOR X!

The pet sim that started it all, this OG experience is a Roblox classic! Start with a cat, dog or rabbit and get to work earning coins by interacting with the environment. It's an incremental sim, which means you'll unlock new levels and powers as you play – so it will keep you entertained for ages! Will you make it far enough to get a titanic pet? They're HUGE!

Best of the rest

Even more worlds to explore!

SWORD FIGHTERS SIMULATOR

Swing your sword (or other weapons) to beat your mates, unlock new weapons and gain immense powers!

GLIDER SIMULATOR

The only thing more fun than soaring through the sky is launching yourself from a cannon and completing mid-air courses!

UNBOXING SIMULATOR

Smash boxes, discover items and collect rewards! This game features hats, pets and some seriously smashing fun.

TOP TIPS

To win at the sims!

1 GREAT GATHER

One of the most important parts of sim games is collecting and earning your income. Never forget to collect these resources (like the coins the animals are grabbing in the picture) as they can be used to grow your projects and increase your success!

2 YOUR TOOLS

Tools are vital to your gameplay in the world of Roblox, and they can range from almost anything, from pillows (as you can see in the picture) to pickaxes. The weapons and tools you're given at the start can often be improved, so keep an eye on your progress and upgrade them as soon as possible. Trust us, the more levelled-up they are, the better!

3 BEE KIND

Although many simulators feature elements of combat, they're mostly very friendly games. Many of the creatures you encounter can actually offer you quests, items and rewards that'll help you out, like this bee in the picture. Remember, you can boss these games by being a friendly player!

TERRIFYING TRIALS

Sometimes all you want is a classic jump scare, and we've totally got you covered. These games bring the fear to Roblox like no others. Are you brave enough to load up these games? If not, maybe skip this chapter!

Try this:
You can pass notes to the other players during the game. If you're a goodie, share your evidence on who could be evil. If you're evil, spread lots of lies!

FLICKER

This fright-fest puts you into a room and assigns you a role. Are you on the good team, the evil team or the neutral team? More importantly, what about everyone else? During each round, the lights will flicker on and off – when they're off, someone will become a victim to the evil team. It's up to everyone to work out who that is!

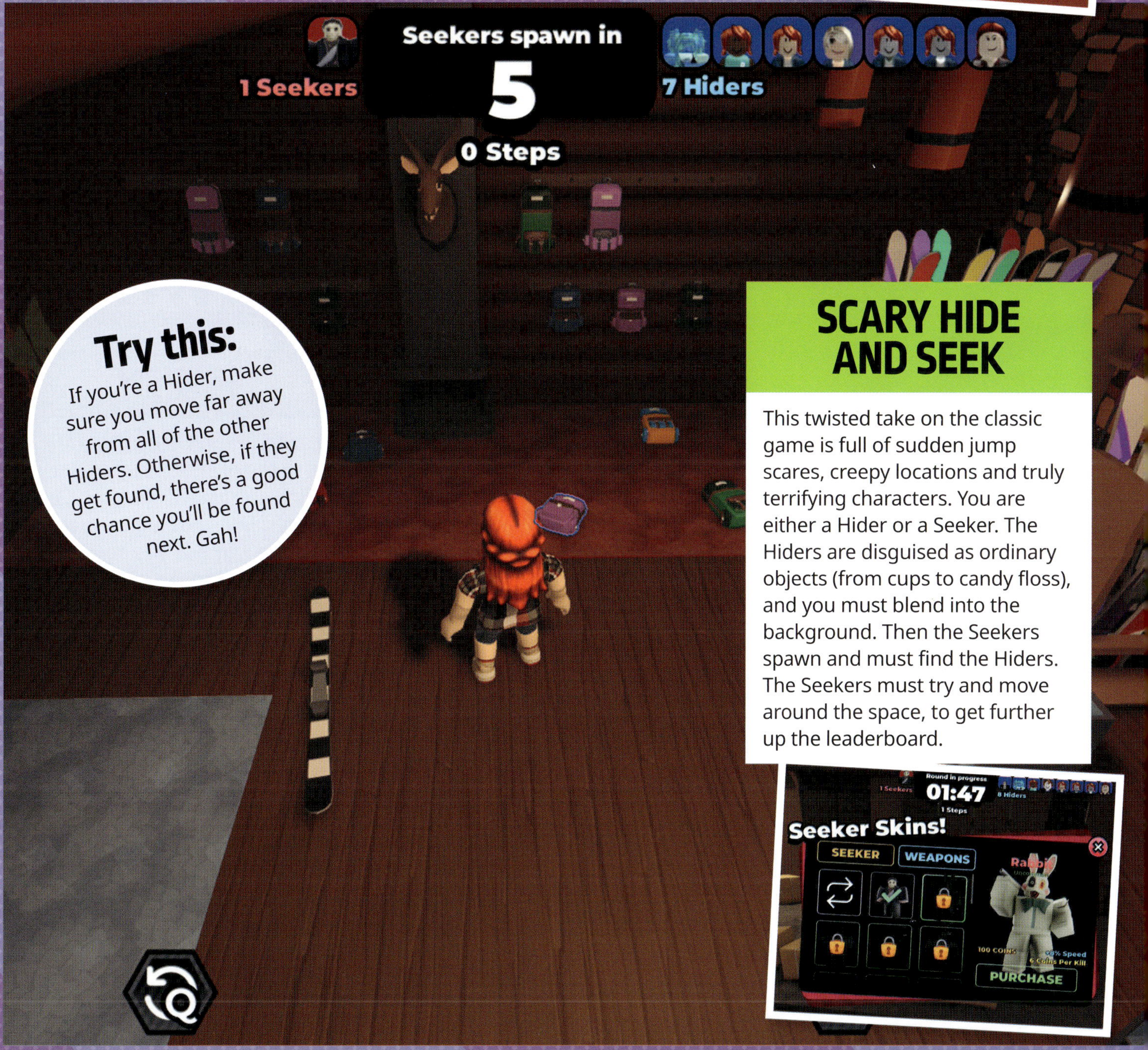

Try this:

If you're a Hider, make sure you move far away from all of the other Hiders. Otherwise, if they get found, there's a good chance you'll be found next. Gah!

SCARY HIDE AND SEEK

This twisted take on the classic game is full of sudden jump scares, creepy locations and truly terrifying characters. You are either a Hider or a Seeker. The Hiders are disguised as ordinary objects (from cups to candy floss), and you must blend into the background. Then the Seekers spawn and must find the Hiders. The Seekers must try and move around the space, to get further up the leaderboard.

DOORS

Doors is set in a spooky hotel, where players must navigate different rooms and find a way to progress, by solving puzzles and unlocking doors. This is easier said than done, when you've got a host of haunted beings with different powers pursuing you! Chapter 1 is in the hotel, but chapter 2 takes you down into some malicious mines. This experience is a Roblox classic!

Try this:

There are daily run challenges to check out! Complete these as fast as you can and you could find a spot on the daily leaderboard.

HAPPY

Walking around a grocery store full of treats after hours is a lot of people's idea of a dream ... but in this game, it's a nightmare! To find a way out, you need to search the store for specific items and scan them at one of three scanners. Sound easy? It isn't, because the store's cleaning robot isn't exactly friendly, and is hunting you down so it can throw you out in the trash. Can you make it out?

Try this:

It's really important to watch your stamina level. This gets used up when you run, so make sure you save your sprints for when you really need to escape trouble!

DANDY'S WORLD

Welcome to the Gardenview Center, an educational building, where you'll take on the role of a cute toon! Aw, how nice! Unfortunately, it's been abandoned by everyone except your squad and a gang of rampaging Twisteds – hostile mascots that want to defeat you. Play as a team, try not to scream and find your way out to survive!

PIGGY

This experience has a whole host of different maps, game modes and items to use as you search for the exit! Unless you're chosen to play as Piggy, in which case your goal is to infect all the other players, which will induct them into your evil team. One player will also be working undercover for Piggy from the start, too. Oink!

Best of the rest

There's nothing like a scream team!

3008

If you found yourself trapped in a furniture store, how would you escape? We suggest you start by building defences against the overnight staff members, who aren't exactly friendly!

CHEESE ESCAPE

There's nothing scary about cheese, is there? Well, in this game, you find yourself in a labyrinth made of cheese. Can you find the way out before the giant rat catches you for dinner?

BACKROOMS

Backrooms is a truly enormous experience, featuring infinite rooms and corridors. To survive, you'll need to complete tricky puzzles and evade the entities that reside here.

TOP TIPS

To survive the night!

1 FEAR FACTOR

These games are designed to scare you, and they probably will – but weapons, tools and items will help. A torch can make any dark space seem much safer ... unless it's beam passes over something scary! What was that?!

2 OUT OF SIGHT

In many horror games, you can simply hide to avoid other players or the game's evil characters. It won't keep you safe forever, but it will buy you extra time to develop a plan ... or to dry your tears. Mwhaha!

3 STRONG SQUAD

Playing on your own as a lone wolf might be a scarier experience, but sticking with your squad gives you strength in numbers and can often increase your chances of survival. Selfishly, it could also cause the enemies to go for someone else instead of you. Yay!

ACTION-PACKED ADVENTURES

If you're looking for the thrill of combat, awesome action and a host of incredible challenges, then these experiences could be your next go-to games. Check out some of our favourites that we've been playing!

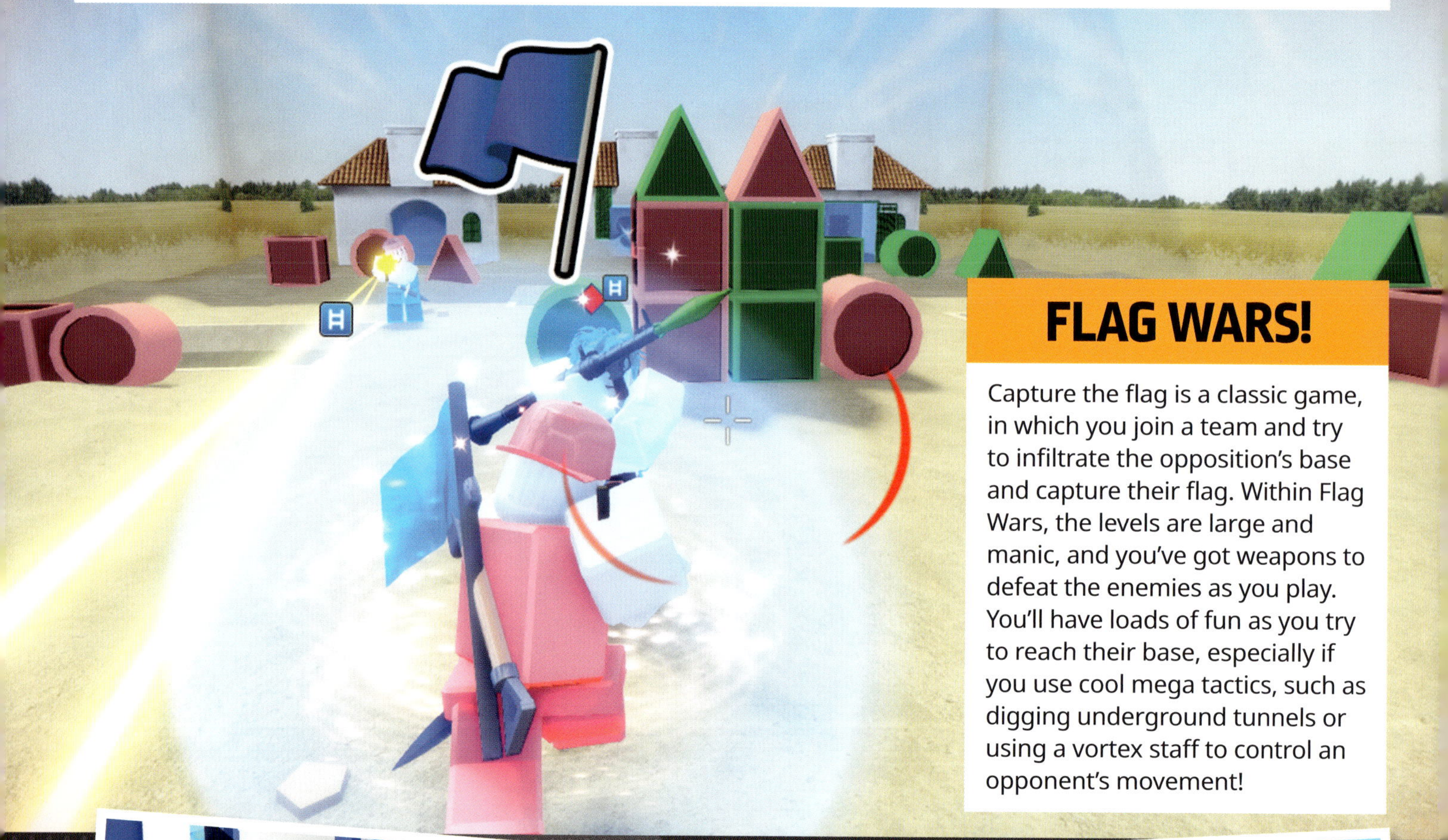

FLAG WARS!

Capture the flag is a classic game, in which you join a team and try to infiltrate the opposition's base and capture their flag. Within Flag Wars, the levels are large and manic, and you've got weapons to defeat the enemies as you play. You'll have loads of fun as you try to reach their base, especially if you use cool mega tactics, such as digging underground tunnels or using a vortex staff to control an opponent's movement!

BLADE BALL

Thanks to its crazy-fast gameplay, Blade Ball has become a viral sensation since it was released in 2023! Set in a big battle arena, there is a huge ball that targets players with increasing speed! You need to run, jump, dodge and parry the ball by hitting it. Timing is key to survival, and the longer your survive, the more unique abilities will be at your disposal!

Try this:
'Curving' is a skill which involves you looking away from the ball or behind it right before hitting it. This makes it harder for your opponents to hit!

BIG PAINTBALL 2!

This paintball sequel is a fast-paced, first-person shooter that is as fun as it is chaotic! You can level up by completing tasks during combat, which enables you to use credit to get your hands on more powerful weapons! Remember, just a single shot can eliminate you from each game, so move carefully and keep your eyes open.

PHANTOM FORCES

Lock and load! It's time for the ultimate in team-based combat. This sensational shooter has two warring factions (the phantoms and the ghosts) and you'll join one as their newest recruit. There are lots of different game modes to try out and even more weapons to master, as you battle your way over incredible landscapes with super-fun themes!

JAILBREAK

It's a classic case of cops vs robbers in this breakout bonanza! If you play as a prisoner, you start with nothing and must find a way to escape the jail and become a criminal on the outside. Meanwhile those playing as police will use all their tools to find criminals and arrest them. Then its straight back to prison to try to escape once again. So much fun!

Best of the rest

Let the adventure begin again!

ANIME DIMENSIONS SIMULATOR

This dungeon crawler takes you straight into the world of anime, as you dash and slash your way through different dimensions based on popular anime!

NINJA LEGENDS

This ninjitsu training simulator requires determination to master the ancient martial arts, and precision to parkour your way up to exciting sky islands!

ZOMBIE RUSH

Wave upon wave of zombies are out for a taste of YOU! Get ready to defend yourself using a host of wicked weapons, or face becoming a zombie yourself!

TOP TIPS

To take on the action!

1 HAPPY ACTION

Are you and your mates feeling a bit tired of playing the same action games? Try taking it in turns suggesting a new game to play – starting with the games from this annual! You can try action games out for the experience, like these players are doing in the picture of Ninja Legends, then stay with your favourites for the laughs!

2 FOLLOW THE LEADER

Action games have a lot of elements to master, so if you're new to these it might be an idea to ask your friend to take the lead on the first game. This way, you can learn all you need to know for next time!

3 IN THE MODE

Most action games involve weapons, items and powers that can enhance your experience. But don't stop there ... Different modes and settings might suit your gameplay more than others, so find out what works for you and play the way you want! In no time, you'll be powering up like this player in Blade Ball!

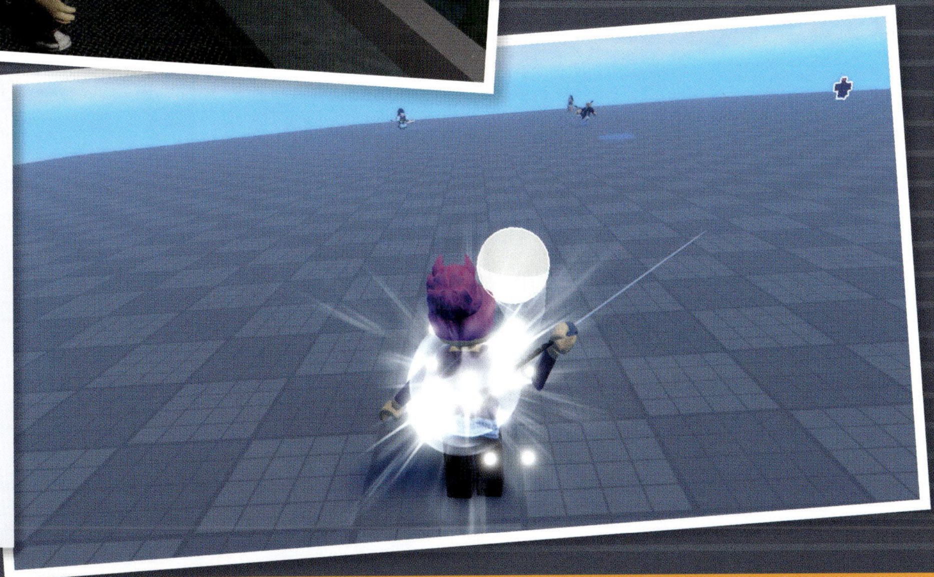

THE ROBLOX RUNWAY

Love fashion, being creative and expressing yourself? Then you've come to the right page! Check out these super stylish games that we're loving at the moment. The runway never looked so good ... or weird!

FASHION FAMOUS

Lights, camera, action – this is your moment to shine in the spotlight! In this experience, you'll need to dress up your avatar in the most impressive outfit and accessories. Each round has a brand-new theme for your creations. The other players will then vote on their favourites and score you. Can you top the fashion charts?

Try this:
Players will judge your fashion, so catch their eye with unexpected creations. Try mixing colours and blending patterns for incredible looks!

CATALOG AVATAR CREATOR

This hugely popular experience is more of a platform than a game! Here, you can equip your avatar with any item from the Roblox Marketplace! Try it on, see what you think and then purchase it later if you love the new look! You can resize, rotate or customise the items, so you can be sure they're the right clothes for you.

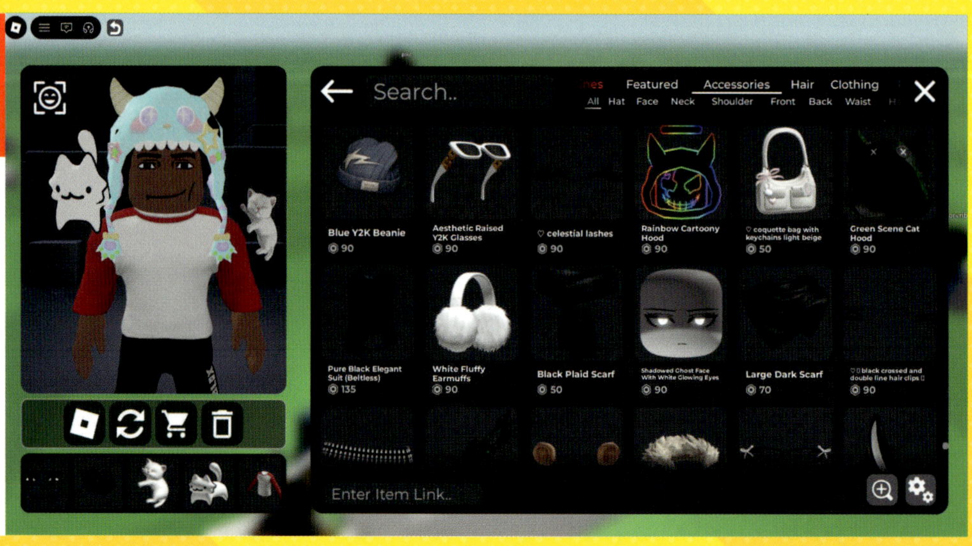

DRESS TO IMPRESS

One of the most popular games on Roblox, Dress to Impress throws you into a fun fashion game show! Create new outfits based on themes, then walk the runway whilst others watch and score your sweet new looks! Suitable for all ages, it's full of friendly fun and competition. Can you go from Newcomer to the rank of Fashion Goddess? There's only one way to find out!

FASHION SHOW

Take on the latest trends and create your dream outfits and style for you and your pets! This is a contest with a twist – you'll be judged on your artistic flair as well as how you strut your stuff on the catwalk! Walk with confidence, strike a pose and wait for the scores to come in. Can you make it to the prestigious winner's podium?

MY SALON TYCOON

The runway isn't all about clothes – people need luscious locks too! In My Salon Tycoon, you can own and operate your own salon or barbershop, and put a smile on the faces of your customers. Earn money by cutting and styling hair, and then hire employees to take on even more work and watch your empire grow and expand!

Best of the rest

More ways to show your fashionable side!

STRUT IN STYLE

Just six minutes separates you from unleashing your beauty brains on the judges. A randomly selected theme, a room full of anticipation – what will you create to become the next top model?

MYTHICAL GUARDIANS

If you want more role-play with your runway, then check out Mythical Guardians. It's an avatar simulation experience in which you'll need to be exploring as much as creating magi-cool looks!

SNEAKER RESELL SIMULATOR

This tycoon game is all about strategy! Buy sneakers and sell them for a profit. Then use this money to open your own sneaker store. You can even unlock advanced gameplay benefits!

TOP TIPS

To look the biz!

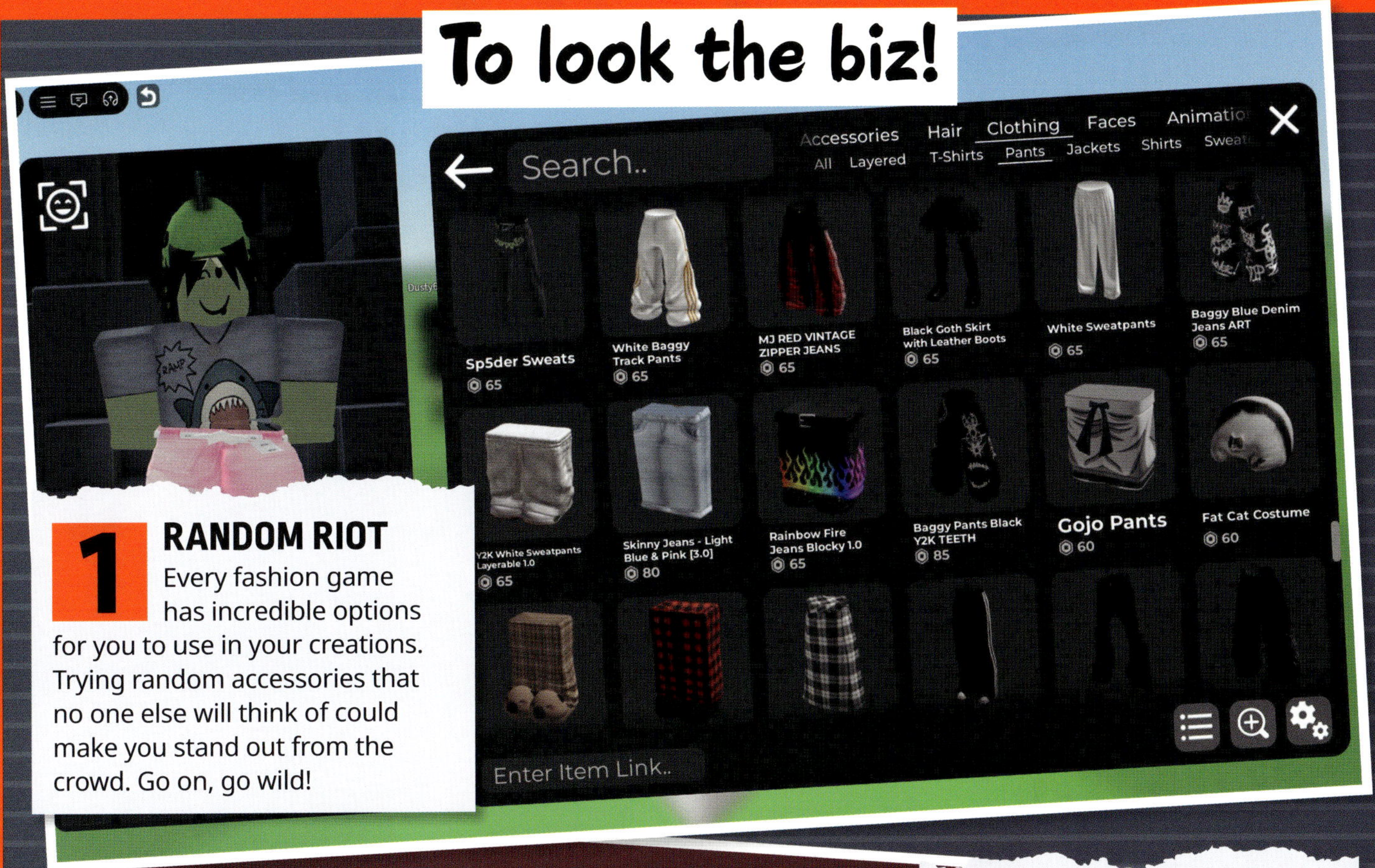

1 RANDOM RIOT

Every fashion game has incredible options for you to use in your creations. Trying random accessories that no one else will think of could make you stand out from the crowd. Go on, go wild!

2 SKILLS ON SHOW

In competitive games, everybody will be showing off their talents. Take note of anything that you think is amazing, and use it later as inspiration to come up with your own unique ideas!

3 CALM AND CUTE

The countdown clock can be a little bit stressful, so our advice is to stay calm and look at all the fashion items on offer, like the player is doing in this picture. This way, you'll feel calmer and more confident when it comes to posing in your new look!

SPORTING TRIUMPHS

The floodlights are shining, the stadium is full and the crowd can be heard for miles around. It's time to lace your boots and race into the world of Roblox sports games!

SUPER STRIKER LEAGUE

This super-speedy football game is legendary within the Roblox community, thanks to its traditional gameplay mixed with incredible power-ups and equipment progression. The matches are five-a-side and full of abilities, like charging your meter to unleash a super strike, or managing your goalkeeper's stamina bar. So rewarding!

Try this:

Look out for items on the pitch. These offer power-ups, like increased speed, higher stamina and even special bombs to stun your opponents!

TPS: STREET SOCCER

Take the beautiful game to the streets with quick-fire passing, delightful dribbling and powerful shots on goal! This sports game is all about your skill levels and how accurately you can time your moves. Advanced moves take some getting the hang of, but they'll be worth it when the crowds are cheering you on!

DUNK A BASKETBALL

Although the controls of this game are simple enough to get to grips with, there's more to the technique than randomly tapping. The only way you'll reach the maximum level of 100 is by perfecting the art of the dunk – and you gain more bounce every second you take in the build up. Collect coins and enchantments and reach for the sky!

SHOCKWAVE RACING

This experience is all about how quickly you can race across randomly-generated obstacle courses. It's one of the fastest games around, and the screen will even shake when you approach max speed! Jump, triple jump, wall run and slide your way to the finish line – but keep an eye on the route ahead and any shortcuts there might be!

VOLLEYBALL LEGENDS

Timing is key to this thumping volleyball experience! Join a team of up to six players, and head to the court to get started. Then get straight to work on the four main controls and when to press the buttons. Once you're feeling confident in your skills, try out the ranked matches!

SUPER GOLF

This game brings the hilarity and fun of mini-golf to Roblox! Compete with your friends and take on a huge selection of themed courses, containing over 240 different holes! The winner is the player who completes a course with the lowest number of strokes! You'll need to master the fine-tune feature to live the dream and get a hole in one!

Best of the rest

Rule more sporting stadiums!

RACKET RIVALS

This intense racket sport is a 3v3 game that is a wonderfully whacky mix of tennis, badminton, squash and volleyball. What's not to love about this smash fest?

TRACK AND FIELD: INFINITE

Jump into these awesome athletic events and see if you can win the gold medal. There's so many cool events to try, such as hurdles and shot put. Go for glory!

SPLASH SKATE & MUSIC

Increase your fame by creating music and performing on stage, then compete in skateboarding missions. They shouldn't work together so well, but they do!

TOP TIPS

To reach sport stardom!

1 CLOSE CONTROL

Most sports games have simple controls, which makes them great for beginners! But the difficulty is in using the controls to perfect your positioning, like the player with the red hair on the pitch is cleverly doing. You'll need to practise switching between the controls to defend well, master the midfield and attack effectively.

2 WATCH AWAY

If you're struggling to get to grips with a sports game, watch how your opponents are playing. If you can work out how they're beating you, practise doing the same and you'll match them in no time!

3 PLAY AS A TEAM

To win a team sports game, you need to first understand the main objectives and how to achieve them. Do you need to defend as a team (like the dyanmic duo behind the net are doing), or attack in numbers? Knowing what to do (and when) can reduce your chances of being caught off guard and defeated!

GOODBYE!

Well there we have it! A whole year's worth of Roblox fun in one awesome book. By now you should have a list of skills you want to unlock and games you want to play – but don't stop there ... there are always new Roblox experiences being released every single day!

Whether you're an obby enthusiast, a sports specialist, a tycoon tyrant or a simulation star, you will always find something fun to try next. Unless you're a new horror fan, in which case you might be too scared to continue ... Oh well, you can stick to the cute and cosy games next time. Play safe and remember to take breaks!

See you next year!

STAYING SAFE ONLINE

YOUNGER FANS' GUIDE

Spending time online is great fun. These games might be your first experience of digital socialising, so here are a few simple rules to help you stay safe and keep the internet an awesome place to spend time:

- Never give out your real name – don't use it as your username.
- Never give out any of your personal details.
- Never tell anybody which school you go to or how old you are.
- Never tell anybody your password, except a parent or guardian.
- Before registering for any account, ask a parent or guardian for permission.
- Take regular breaks, as well as playing with parents nearby, or in shared family rooms.
- Always tell a parent or guardian if something is worrying you.

PARENTS' GUIDE

ONLINE CHAT
In most games, there is live on-screen text chat between users. Parents are advised to ensure that their children are only talking to friends and that they aren't being exposed to any adult matter.

SOUND
Sound is crucial in many video games. Players will often wear headphones, meaning parents won't be able to hear what children are listening to. Set up your console or computer to have sound coming from the TV or monitor as well as the headset, so you can hear what your child is experiencing.

REPORTING PLAYERS
If you see or hear a player being abusive, Roblox allows you to report users or interactions. You'll be able to use the Report Abuse links found throughout the site on game pages, but there may also be buttons within chat windows or game menus where you can raise a case with community managers.

SCREEN TIME
Taking regular breaks is important.
Set play sessions by using a timer.
Some games can last a long time and if your child finishes playing in the middle of a round, they could leave their teammates a player short, and lose any points they've earned. It is advisable to give an advanced warning for stopping play or clearly outlining a stopping point before any play session begins.

IN-GAME PURCHASES
Many games offer in-app purchases to enhance the game experience, but they're not required to play the game. They also don't improve a player's performance. There are ways to set up safety measures on you child's account by setting up a PIN through Settings. Consult these before allowing your child to play any game in order to avoid any unpermitted spending on your account.